Where It Stops, Nobody Knows

AMY · EHRLICH
Where It Stops, Nobody Knows

Dial Books for Young Readers

New York

Published by Dial Books for Young Readers
A Division of NAL Penguin Inc.
2 Park Avenue
New York, New York 10016

Published simultaneously in Canada
by Fitzhenry & Whiteside Limited, Toronto
Copyright © 1988 by Amy Ehrlich
All rights reserved
Printed in the U.S.A.
Design by Amelia Lau Carling

(b)
2 3 4 5 6 7 8 9 10

Library of Congress Cataloging in Publication Data
Ehrlich, Amy, 1942–
Where it stops, nobody knows / by Amy Ehrlich.
p. cm.
Summary: Nina and her mother move from place
to place, never revealing anything of themselves,
and causing Nina to wonder if they will
ever stop hiding.
ISBN 0-8037-0575-1
[1. Mothers and daughters—Fiction.] I. Title.
PZ7.E328Jo 1988 [Fic]—dc19 88-4095 CIP AC

*To Sarah Draney
and Theresa Del Pozzo*

*I would like to thank
Emily Abel, Nancy Lamb, Michael Ingraham, Bill Gray,
Xenia Williams, and Ann and Shannon Lemmon
for their help during the writing of this book.*

Where It Stops, Nobody Knows

✔ Part One

Montpelier, Vermont

1 It was sunny the first time we saw Montpelier. If it had been cloudy or rainy, we probably would have driven right by. But as it was, the sight of that gold dome sparkling like crazy next to the narrow little river made Joyce roll down her window and hit the brakes. "What do you say we try this town, kiddo?" she asked me.

She wasn't talking about a short visit either. The back of our Chevy van was packed solid and we'd been on the road for more than a month, which is how long it takes to get to Vermont from Fairbanks, Alaska, if only one person drives. We'd been planning to move to Boston, but I didn't care. I was sick of traveling, and besides, every other kid my age was in school.

Joyce parked the car in a lot. We had to lock Silky in the van, but she was used to it. We left the windows open a couple of inches so she could get some air and walked down the main street of the town. It was pretty, I'll admit that. Almost all the buildings were red brick and there were plenty of trees—Joyce said they were maples—with red and orange and yellow leaves.

A small bridge crossed over a back street and we found a restaurant to have lunch in. It was some kind of health food restaurant, but it smelled good when we walked in, like apples maybe or bread baking. We sat down at a table next to the steamy plate-glass windows and a waitress wearing a beautiful homemade sweater handed us menus.

I was reading mine, thinking I'd have some soup du jour, when Joyce suddenly got up and walked over to the counter where the waitresses were working. I saw her talking to them, using her hands a lot the way she does when she's excited, and as soon as she came back to the table I was sure something was up. "You got a job," I said. A wild guess, but not really if you know Joyce.

"Breakfast and lunch," she said. "I start on Monday. It'll be perfect. I'll be through by the time you get home from school."

"What home? What school?" I asked her. The truth is that Joyce has a tendency to not think things through very well. I'm much better organized, even though she's the mother and I'm the kid. When it's just the two of you, those kinds of differences become clearer. Joyce really counts on me to keep track of a lot of things, and it's *made* me more organized. I feel sorry for kids who get treated like they have only half a brain.

Of course experience helps too. God knows I've had plenty of that. I can't even tell you how many places Joyce and I have lived in, but it's something like fourteen states so far plus Toronto, Canada. None of the places were right for us, that's all.

Even though I'd made fun of Joyce for being excited about getting a job before we'd found a place to live, still it did seem like a good sign. The waitress brought my soup. It was a delicious creamy chowder. My insides got warm as I ate and I thought about the gold dome down by the river. Maybe if nothing bad happened, we'd be able to stay in Montpelier.

It turns out that that building is the state capitol. Every winter people come from all the towns in Vermont and meet to talk about new laws they should make. Most of them leave their families behind, but sometimes they don't. That's good, Joyce said, because it makes the school used to dealing with new kids. They don't have a problem with it.

The Montpelier middle school was called the Main Street School. Joyce found out where it was (on Main Street, of course) and she took me to register the morning after we came in to town. So what if we'd slept in the van? School was more important than anything as far as Joyce was concerned, so she set the alarm clock and made me wash up in the rest room at the Mini-Mart where we got coffee and milk and doughnuts to go.

But we were still half an hour late. As we walked down the dim hallway, I could hear teachers giving lessons. Laughter came from behind one door. In the office there was a secretary, as well as a couple of teachers who were drinking coffee and grading papers. The principal was away on a trip. No one seemed too concerned. All they wanted were my Fairbanks records, they didn't ask for anything earlier—which was a good thing since we didn't have them.

"I'll meet you outside right after school," said Joyce. And she gave me a wink for luck. Actually I wasn't at all nervous. If you've been a new kid as many times as I have, you wouldn't be nervous either. I always figure that kids at school are basically bored and don't have enough to think about. So even though a person they've never seen might be a big deal in the beginning, the novelty usually wears off in a few weeks. Plus I know how to blend in. I'm kind of like a chameleon in that way—I adopt protective coloring.

For example, at this school I could tell right away that kids were behind the kids in Fairbanks in fashion. Probably that's because Fairbanks is a bigger city with lots of shopping centers and malls. Only one or two kids in my class even looked punk. The rest were either preppy or else just wore cheap poor-looking clothes.

One thing that's really wonderful about Joyce is that no matter how tight money is, she'll always buy me whatever clothes I want. And she lets me wear makeup to school. Today I hadn't put it on because I wanted to see whether the other girls wore it. At least five or six did so that was great.

The teacher was talking to me. She was handing me some books. I stopped my inspection of the kids and tried to pay attention to what she was saying. What was her name? If anyone had told it to me, I'd forgotten.

As far as the work went, it was fairly easy. They were studying the thirteen colonies, which I'd already had twice—once in fourth grade when we lived in Denver and last year in Fairbanks. History and English are my best subjects anyway. Whatever I read is completely vivid in my mind—I can see the people moving around, going through their days. Even if they lived long ago when America was still a wilderness, I figure they were pretty much like me.

Math is harder for me, I'll admit it. It's weird, too, because I have no trouble understanding money and maps and things that involve numbers. But in this school for once I was lucky. My seventh-grade teacher in Fairbanks had been a math fanatic and by the time the year was half over, he had us doing eighth-grade work. So even though I'd gotten a D the final marking period, here I was multiplying and dividing fractions at lightning speed, no problem.

Of course you don't ever want to be too smart. That's a mistake. Kids don't like anyone who's too smart, and also it makes the teacher notice you. I remember once when we were living in Seattle—we lived there for a few months before we went to Fairbanks—I wrote this composition on fireflies. It was about how their lights keep you company in the dusk, coming out one by one, or were the lights there all along and it took the dusk to see them? My teacher thought it was great. She gave me a prize and made me read it out loud, first in assembly and then at a school board meeting. But Joyce had been really annoyed when she found out. "If I want a celebrity in the family, I'll go on television," she'd said.

Chairs were rattling around me. It was the end of the period and kids were going to lunch. This was the hardest time for me. Everyone was in the middle of their ongoing dramas with one another, but I had no part in it yet. I looked around, wondering who would be my friend. There was one girl who reminded me of myself. She had red hair like mine and she was wearing a pleated skirt and a pink sweatshirt with a picture of palm trees and the ocean on it. I thought she looked original.

I followed her downstairs to the cafeteria, willing her to turn around and see that I was there. Then I took a tray and followed her through the lunch line. Beef stew, noodles, Jell-O salad, milk. It all looked pretty disgusting. "This looks pretty disgusting," I said. No answer.

We got to the end of the line and I was amazed to see a cashier. I felt in my jacket pockets for money but of course there wasn't any. Joyce and I hadn't thought about it, that's all. For one wild moment I considered asking the girl in front of me if I could borrow some money. But she had already paid for her food and was going over to a large table where three other girls were waving to her. They were all wearing sweatshirts with pictures on them. So much for originality. I left my tray where it was and walked out of the cafeteria.

"You should have given me money for lunch," I told Joyce after school.

"You should have asked me for it," said Joyce. "Since when have you stopped thinking for yourself?"

We were walking down the street with Silky on her leash. The sky was overcast and leaves were flying through the air. Silky was the only one in a good mood. Her tail was up and she looked almost like she was prancing. I guess she was glad to get out of the van.

"It's just this one more apartment I want to look at," said Joyce, holding up a page from the newspaper. "Maybe if they actually see Silky, she'll win them over." The building we'd come to was a wood-frame house, gray with white trim. It had a big front porch, a slate roof, and gable windows on the second floor. It was like a house I had dreamed up. It was that perfect.

Joyce knocked on the door and I crossed my fingers behind my back. You have no idea how prejudiced people all over America are against dogs. What have dogs ever done to them? I asked Joyce that once and her answer was "Plenty!" If it weren't for me, Joyce would never have a dog. But she feels guilty about being such a small family, so she finally let me get Silky three years ago. We thought Silky was a golden retriever, but she turned out to be a mutt.

"Sit, Silky," I said in my sternest voice.

The woman who came to the door must have been cooking supper. She had on an apron and was drying her hands on a dish towel. She looked old, in her sixties at least.

"We've come about the apartment," said Joyce. "Do you allow animals?"

"I don't see why not, so long as they don't bark at night or dig up my lawn," said the woman, putting down her dish towel and leading us upstairs. As she showed us the apartment, I had an impression of old-fashioned wallpaper and lots of dark wood. But the thing I noticed that day turned out to be what really sold Joyce on Montpelier. Like the waitresses in the restaurant and the secretary at my school, the landlady didn't ask us any questions. Not a single one.

2

It was snowing. Big wet flakes fell all around me and melted on the sidewalk. I was on my way to meet Joyce at work. We were going to have dinner at the restaurant and then go to the movies. I was glad we planned it this morning, otherwise I'd be depressed. I always get like this at the beginning of winter.

Actually it's not the snow I mind, it's the darkness. Today when I got out of intramurals, it was dark for the first time. I hate that. In my opinion, they should just have daylight savings time all year long. It's so awful when night starts at four in the afternoon. Of course in Fairbanks it was much worse. I keep asking Joyce why we can't move to a sunny place like Atlanta or Miami, but she refuses. She hates the South. She says she suffers too much from the heat.

When I walked into the restaurant, a little bell tinkled on the door. They must have it to let them know when customers come in. As it was, the place was almost empty. Three women sat in the back, talking softly with the newspaper spread open on the table. No waitresses were in sight. I sat down and took my science book out of my backpack. We were having a test tomorrow. I figured that Joyce was probably in the kitchen and she'd be right out.

I don't know how long I sat there. At one point I actually put my head down on the table and closed my eyes. I heard the bell on the door tinkle and when I woke up, Joyce was sitting across the table. "You seemed tired, so I decided to let you sleep," she said, smiling at me.

"You mean you knew I was here?"

"Of course. Didn't you see me? I was at that back table with Dinah and Patty."

"Who are they?"

"The other waitresses. You want to meet them?"

Now this was really unusual. Joyce hardly ever talks about the rest of her life away from me, much less lets me meet anyone. I don't mean we aren't close, it's just that we respect each other's privacy. Besides, most of Joyce's jobs haven't been that great. She worked as a taxi dispatcher in Seattle and in a print shop in Fairbanks. Before that she was mainly an office temp, but she never wanted to learn keyboarding so that was the end of that. I honestly think working in this restaurant is the happiest she's been in a while. At least she seems more peaceful.

"Take your backpack and I'll introduce you," she said. "We can sit with them." We walked to the back of the restaurant. I saw Joyce fluff her hair with her fingers and it occurred to me that she was nervous. I wasn't sure why though. She should know by this time that I could handle myself no matter what.

"Is there another chair for my daughter?" she asked. "This is Nina."

She'd forgotten to tell me their names. Great. One was Dinah and one was Patty but which was which? I concentrated on their faces. Actually I'm a pretty good judge of grown-ups, and these women seemed all right. Both of them were big women—not fat really, but you know what I mean. They wore long skirts and high boots and you could tell by their clothing and just by the way they were that you'd never be bored by their company. I had the idea that they probably weren't from Montpelier. Or at least they didn't look like the people you ordinarily saw on the streets.

One of the women, the older one, stood up and handed me a menu. "What would you like to eat? The chili's good."

"I think I'll have the chili."

"Wise choice."

As we ate, the restaurant began filling up for dinner. Some businessmen came in and a few families with little kids sat at big tables. Patty and Dinah kept jumping up to get them things. But each time they came back they said, "Now where were we?" and the conversation went right on. I felt privileged to be sitting with the waitresses and I remembered the first time we'd come here, just ourselves, and not a part of anything at all.

The two of them really wanted to know about me. They asked all the regular questions about what grade I was in and what subjects I had, but then they asked other questions too, like how it felt to move so much. Everything I said, they would take between them like two dogs with a bone.

"Have you worked together for a long time?" I asked them finally. I was getting tired of being the one to talk and I could see Joyce looking at me, probably wondering if I'd say the right thing.

"Oh, goodness. It's been far too long!" the younger woman said. "I hate to think—"

"Six and half years. That's not *that* long, Dinah."

Well at least now I knew which one was which.

"We opened up on Memorial Day," continued Dinah. "We ran out of everything in an hour and a half. It's amazing we're still open."

"You mean this is your place? You don't just work here?"

Joyce pushed aside her dinner. "I told you that, Nina. I'm sure I did."

Fat chance! She hadn't even told me they existed. "I guess I must have forgotten. Sorry," I said.

"In my opinion you look just like your mother. That fabulous red hair," said Patty, touching her own head. Her hair looked fine to me, even though it did have a lot of gray in it. I certainly wasn't about to tell her that Joyce's came out of a bottle. Her real color was dark brown. It was one of the things about herself that Joyce really truly hated. Since she wouldn't go to a beauty parlor, I helped her put a red rinse in it once a month. And then sometimes she would give me a perm.

"Do you have boyfriends here yet?" Dinah asked me.

"No, not really." Even if I did, I wasn't about to tell them, that was for sure!

"Boys have always liked Nina," said Joyce. "But I think she'd rather not talk about it."

"Joyce understands me," I said, trying to make it into a joke when actually she'd just told them to mind their own business. I felt Dinah and Patty looking at us with complete fascination, their mouths slightly open.

"Have you always called her Joyce?" asked Patty. "If my kids ever called me Patty, my husband would have a fit."

I looked at my watch. Joyce refused to wear one so it was my job to get us moving. "It's ten to eight, Joyce. The movie starts at ten after."

"Right," said Joyce and she got our coats off the coatrack. I was ready to leave anyway. I felt like I wanted to be outdoors in the chilly air. The restaurant seemed too hot or maybe it was just that the oven was on.

"Thanks for the supper," said Joyce. I wondered if she'd pay like other customers but nobody gave us a bill. Well I guess it was part of her wages.

Patty walked us to the door and held it open like

we were company who'd come to visit. "Come back again soon, Nina. I kept wanting to meet you. I made your mother promise to bring you in."

As Joyce and I walked down the street to the movie theater, neither of us said a word. The snow was falling steadily now. It glittered under the streetlights. For maybe the millionth time in my life I wished that Joyce and I were more like everyone else. Or at least that we could *appear* to be like everyone else.

Take those women, Dinah and Patty. They were unusual too, you could see it easily, smarter probably and more enterprising than most people. But even if they'd moved here from another place, even if their parents and sisters and brothers lived far away, they *had* them, I was sure of that, and husbands and children too. But for Joyce and me there was no backdrop of grandparents or families or people who'd always known us. Sometimes that made everything seem so fragile I could hardly stand it.

When we got there, the movie theater was quiet—the candy stand wasn't even open. I guess the snow had kept people at home. After we'd bought our tickets and were waiting for the movie to begin, I brought up the subject of Dinah and Patty. "I thought those women were really nosy," I said as though we'd just been discussing it.

"Who?"

"Patty and Dinah. *You* know."

Joyce took off her jacket. For a moment I was afraid

she wasn't going to say anything. "I like them. They're curious about us, that's all."

I'm not sure why, but what she said seemed like a criticism of me. Did she think I didn't like her to have friends or something? I *loved* it that she might have friends. *I* always did in the places we lived. That was kind of my specialty, making friends. And one part of my mind secretly held out the idea that if Joyce ever found what she was looking for in one place, we could stay there forever. Friends? Isn't that what everyone wanted?

The lights in the theater dimmed and the movie credits came on the screen. It was an old movie, *The Sailor Who Fell from Grace with the Sea.* The story was about a boy my age who spied on his mother in her bedroom. It was truly weird. The boy was part of a gang who did sadistic things to animals. From almost the first scene you knew something just terrible was going to happen. I sat there squirming in my seat, and after the gang dissected a cat and the boy's mother took Kris Kristofferson as her lover, Joyce grabbed my hand and whispered, "Let's get out of here." Was I ever relieved! Neither of us can stand suspense. If anything, Joyce hates it even more than I do.

We left the theater and raced home through the empty, snowy streets. I'd left the lights on in our apart-ment and it looked like we were the only ones still awake on our block. Often it was that way. I don't have a bedtime or anything, and some nights I'll sit by the windowsill and feel like Joyce and I are the only people left alive in the world.

Tonight neither of us was tired, so Joyce made some tea while I took Silky out for a fast walk. As soon as we came onto the front step, Silky's ears stuck straight up. If dogs could grin, she'd be grinning. Naturally she loved the snow. You'd think she'd never seen it before, the way she lifted it up with her nose and ran around in circles. "Come on, Silky, I don't have all night," I told her. And then she peed, just like that. Silky is one smart dog, no question about it.

When we came back upstairs, Joyce had put an old jazz tape on—I think it was Ella Fitzgerald—and she was sitting on the living room rug, drinking tea and working on a hat for me. She was always knitting me something, scarves or mittens or hats. I already had more of these than I needed, but Joyce said she liked to keep her hands busy. She never made anything for herself.

If you were to peek through our window into this apartment (or any of our apartments, for that matter), you'd probably be surprised. In the first place there's hardly any furniture. Just mattresses for Joyce and me, a folding table and chair, and big suitcases for our clothing. Who needs to haul around major furniture like bureaus and couches? What's the point? Yet we have rugs in every room and drawings and posters on the walls.

All my life, or at least as long as I can remember, I've collected pictures of sunsets. I buy postcards of sunsets and I cut photographs of sunsets out of magazines like *National Geographic*. In each place I make an entirely new collage of sunset pictures for my room, adding the newer ones and putting some old ones away.

Joyce's pictures are different of course. She has lots of framed posters of famous old paintings that even have glass on them. It's a real pain packing those and moving them, I can tell you, but Joyce really values them. Those paintings and her plants are her most precious possessions.

As soon as we arrive in a new town, one of the first things Joyce does is hit the five-and-ten or the supermarket and buy a lot of African violets and other flowering plants. She puts them on the windowsills of whatever apartment we have and watches over them as if they were babies the whole time we live there. The only part that seems weird to me is what she does with them in the end. She throws them out.

"Have you finished your homework yet?" Joyce asked me. "Would you like some tea?"

I told her "No," and "Yes," and brought my books over to the kitchen table. Joyce put the kettle back on to boil and Silky stretched and yawned and fell asleep next to my feet. "There's a small hotel with a wishing well," sang Ella Fitzgerald in her deep, sweet voice.

It was nearly eleven and the moon was shining in the window. At that moment I would not have traded places with anyone.

3   I have to admit that my life as a kid at the Main Street School was beginning to look up. The reason was weird, something completely out of the blue. I'm tall, almost five seven, and I've always been fast. I hate team sports, but basketball is their big winter sport in Vermont, and at this school, girls' basketball was even bigger than boys'. I don't think they'd lost a game in five years. From almost my first day everyone was after me to go out for it. The way it worked was that first you had intramurals and then in December you went out for the traveling team.

All the best kids played basketball. It wasn't like in Fairbanks or plenty of other places, where it was every kid for themselves. Montpelier seemed old-fashioned in that way. Joyce said it reminded her of the 1950's; to me it was like that movie *Back to the Future*. Your school was everything. There were even cheerleaders for the *girls'* team.

The basketball coach was the same for both boys and girls. He was the seventh-grade history teacher, but people also said he played Division I in college.

He was the tallest man I'd ever seen—six ten at least. You had to hold your head way back to see him. His name was Fred Jenks.

From the first day we had intramurals, this guy was really on my case. I was there mainly just to be with kids. I was lonely, it was as simple as that. But he was determined to make me a center. Me, who'd never even played! "Okay, Lewis, keep moving. Take those long arms and grab that ball. What are you waiting for? My last center never played before either and she made all-state." How could you say no to someone like that? Forget it!

But after the first couple of weeks, I began to know more what to do. I pumped with my legs, and reached and swiveled with my arms and shoulders. I ran down the court, staying alert and waiting for someone to pass me the ball. In almost every case that person was Casey Allen, power forward. She was my height or taller and after a while people began to call us "the twin towers," after the two big skyscrapers in New York City.

I liked having a nickname even if it was a shared one. And even though I might not have picked Casey as a friend, she had some good virtues, such as she was very calm. Cool under pressure. I like to think of myself that way too. Just last week I'd started eating lunch with Casey and some other girls she sat with every day. It was better than sitting alone, I'll tell you that. Eighth-grade girls can be *cold*.

In the younger grades it was different. They had clubs with secret names, but at least you knew about them. If you were out, you knew it. But for the past few years—since sixth grade, I'd say—boys were involved and they changed everything.

I remember noticing this for the first time when we were living in Pittston, Pennsylvania, a place that truly lived up to its name. Me and three other girls had a club we called the Rectangle Club. Once a week we went out for ice cream sodas. Big deal! But actually it was fun in its way, we'd try a new flavor each time. But then two of the girls started liking the same boy. They were so mean to each other, I hated it.

In Montpelier as far as I could tell, there were very few couples. People mainly did things in groups. That's why it was important to *be* in a group in the first place. Otherwise you'd have absolutely no access to boys. For example, the first weekend after I'd started really hanging out with Casey Allen, Jenny Bouchard, another girl at our lunch table, invited everyone to a party. "It's just going to be the good athletes, you know what I mean," she said. That was part of the invitation.

I was really excited. I already liked this one boy, Sam Gordon. He was only about five three or four, and skinny, but he was an incredible basketball player. His moves were amazing! He'd just moved to Montpelier like me, but he'd started school at the beginning of the year. I heard he used to live in Chicago and

had learned to play basketball from Black kids and
Puerto Ricans.

I never said a word about Sam to anyone else. I was
worried that the other girls were already my rivals.
How could they not like Sam when to me he was so
exceptional? It wasn't like I was planning a big se-
duction anyway. I just wanted to *watch* Sam at Jenny's
party. I was after information, that's all, something I
could think about at night before I fell asleep. Did he
like potato chips or Fritos? What would he wear to a
party? Did he dance?

The party was supposed to be at eight on Saturday
night. Casey lived in town like me and she said her
parents could take us if mine would pick us up. Now
all I had to do was persuade Joyce to let me go. She
could be funny about things like parties, undependa-
ble. Sometimes all I got was a flat no, other times she'd
go through a big routine of calling up the kid's parents
and making sure they'd be home. I only remember
once in Fairbanks when she'd said yes, no questions
asked.

It was strange when you stopped to think about it
because in some ways Joyce was fairly loose. Maybe
she was worried about my safety. She said she was.
But then she'd let me do other things—things I think
are *more* dangerous, like going horseback riding and
making the horses gallop. Who knows? And in a way,
who cares? The main part was that I had to get her
to say yes about Jenny's party.

When I got home from school, I saw there was another car parked in the driveway, some kind of Japanese car, a Subaru or a Nissan. But I didn't think too much about it until I came upstairs. There at our kitchen table, making the room seem all filled up somehow, was Patty. I looked around but at first I didn't see Joyce anywhere. I couldn't exactly say "What are you doing here?" so I just stood at the door with my mouth open.

"Hi, Nina. Don't you look nice. Did Joyce knit you that hat?"

"Yes," I said. "Where is she?"

Patty laughed. "She was right here a minute ago. Look in the next room."

Just then Joyce walked in. "I don't think I heard you say hello to Patty," she said. I felt embarrassed to be criticized in front of someone else.

"Oh, that's okay," Patty said. "I know what it's like to have only one thing on your mind."

She was certainly right about that. And it suddenly came to me that this might be a good time to bring up Jenny Bouchard's party. I just had a feeling that Joyce would not say no with Patty there. Patty liked to seem on my side, I'm not sure why.

I got myself an apple from the refrigerator and sat down with her. Joyce was still standing in the doorway. "Do you know a family named the Bouchards?" I asked Patty.

"Paul Bouchard? He works for legal aid?"

"I don't know, but they have a daughter named Jenny, she's in my class. Can I go to her party, Joyce? It's tomorrow night in East Montpelier. Casey Allen's parents can drive us if you can pick us up. All the kids are going."

Joyce looked over at Patty. "Where have I heard that line before?" The answer was nowhere, because I'd never said it, but maybe she was just trying to seem like a normal mother to Patty. "Oh, all right," she said then. "But I'll have to call this girl's parents, and I want you home no later than eleven."

"Eleven-thirty. Please, Joyce. The party doesn't even start till eight."

"We'll see," said Joyce. "Maybe."

She made some tea then and everybody seemed more comfortable. I asked Patty about her kids. They were all much older than me; two were already married and the youngest one was in college. I'd say Patty and Joyce were about the same age, but Joyce didn't have me until she was thirty-five so she was the one who was unusual.

I've always thought that Joyce's being so old when I was born explained a lot of things. Mainly, although she's never said this, I think she got pregnant on purpose. She wasn't married to my father when I was born. I doubt if she ever even saw him again after she got pregnant. He was a lawyer she met in a bar in Catskill, New York, when she was working as a waitress. I think it was very simple. She was thirty-five years old and she really wanted a baby. She wanted me then and she loves me like crazy now. In spite of everything, I've never doubted that.

Casey Allen's father was twenty minutes late. I'd made Joyce let me wait for them outside and by the time they came my feet were about frozen. All I had on were stockings and flats—and my other clothes too, of course. Well, I wasn't going to wear big rubber boots to a party.

The three of us sat in the front seat of their car and listened to country and western music on the radio. They had a big old-fashioned Mercury and it seemed to just glide along the curves in the road. If I was lucky, Sam Gordon would talk to me at the party. But even if he didn't, I was with a friend my own age going at night to a place I'd never been before. My heart pounded happily.

Jenny's house was way out in the country, high on a hill. There were other dark shapes around it and when we got up close I realized they were barns. I never would have thought Jenny lived on a farm. She had the nicest clothes of almost anyone in our class.

Inside everyone was watching television. It was actually a movie, *Nightmare on Elm Street*. How was I going to handle this when I couldn't even sit through *The Sailor Who Fell from Grace with the Sea*? The whole downstairs of the house was dim, with people crammed on the couches and the television flickering. The movie music sounded like someone was stalking some-one else to kill them. I left.

The next room was the kitchen. When I walked in, the only person I saw was Sam Gordon. Amazing! He was leaning against the dishwasher, drinking a Coke. "You don't like horror movies either?" he asked me. Each of us knew who the other one was, although we'd never met. (I, of course, *really* knew who he was.) Up close I could see that his skin was incredibly smooth and that he had brown eyes, so dark they were almost black. He was much handsomer than I thought.

I tried to remember what he'd said so that we could have a conversation. Horror movies, that was it. "I hate them," I said. "I never go to them."

"That's too bad. After *Nightmare on Elm Street*, I think Jenny told me they had *Psycho II* and *Friday the Thirteenth*."

"You're kidding."

"Right, I'm kidding."

"Are you kidding?"

"No, I'm serious."

Both of us laughed and sat down on a couch that was in the kitchen. On a table in front of it were bowls of chips and pretzels and cans of soda, all different kinds. I helped myself to a Sprite. And then I thought that maybe Sam Gordon was only sitting there because he didn't want to be rude and leave. In a way I'd rather he *would* leave. I didn't have too many hopes of things like this working out for me. They just tended not to, that's all.

Sam didn't say another word and I began rehearsing sentences in my head, but none of them sounded natural to me. Maybe I could talk to him about our two basketball teams. But just then the lights went on in the other room and I heard a lot of screeching and giggling. The next thing I knew Casey and another girl, Lynn Cutter, had come into the kitchen.

"What's to eat?" said Casey.

"What's going on in there?" asked Sam.

"Oh, you know. The usual stuff."

I had no idea what they meant, but it turned out that lots of kids had been making out while the movie was on. Some were even in the bedrooms. That seemed surprising in a way, but it really didn't interest me. All I could think about was Sam Gordon. Why had I acted like such a shy jerk?

The rest of the party seemed to move by me in slow motion. I noticed Sam all the time without ever looking at him directly. It was weird. But the worst part was that I could tell Lynn Cutter liked him too. She managed to stay around him and she sat next to him during the next movie. But it wasn't *Psycho II*. For some strange reason they'd gotten *The Sound of Music* and everyone sang along with the characters.

By the time Joyce picked Casey and me up at eleven-thirty, I was so frustrated and sad, I couldn't even talk in the van home. I'd been worrying about this trip all afternoon, wondering how Joyce would act in front of Casey, but because of Sam Gordon, it didn't seem to matter to me anymore. Joyce was Joyce, and there was nothing I could do about it. If Casey didn't like her, too bad.

4 "What are you doing for Christmas?" asked Jenny Bouchard.

It was the last day before school vacation and we were throwing our books into our lockers. A picture of Jenny's farm, surrounded by snow, came into my mind. They probably had it decorated with candles in every window.

What was I supposed to say? Usually Joyce and I gave each other some presents and went for a walk. Once we had dinner in a fancy restaurant.

Christmas is supposed to be so important, but a lot of people really suffer at that time of year, I think. Take Joyce for example. She'll always try to make a nice day for me, but unlike me she has other people from her past, family who she must remember and miss. My grandparents both died when she was only twenty, and Joyce and her one brother lost track of each other because we've moved around so much. A few years ago she wrote him a letter to his old address in upstate New York and it came back saying he'd moved, address unknown.

Jenny clanged her locker door shut and walked away. Now she'd *know* I was weird. I'd never even answered her.

I walked home from school slowly. Joyce had started working two nights a week and she wouldn't be home till late. I thought I'd go downtown so that I could look in the shop windows. As I walked over the Granite Street Bridge, I could hear music—"God Rest Ye Merry Gentlemen," I think it was—being broadcast from one of the churches. It was a warm hazy afternoon with snow melting on the sidewalks and dripping off the roofs. I bought myself an ice cream cone and strolled along, wondering what to buy Joyce for Christmas. A street vendor on one corner had some really nice hats with ear flaps and designs woven into them.

The problem was I only had about twenty cents left of my lunch money. Joyce didn't believe in allowance. Usually when I asked her for money, she just gave it to me, as much as I wanted. Maybe tonight I'd tell her I needed new sneakers or something.

"How much are those hats?" I asked the vendor, pointing to the one I liked.

"Twelve dollars. They're all wool." He handed me the hat so that I could feel it. The colors were purples and greens with a border of bright blue. Joyce would love this hat.

"Will you be here tomorrow?"

"No, just today. Tomorrow we'll be in Barre."

Joyce's restaurant was two blocks away. I could go there and get the money from her. "Okay," I told the vendor. "Don't sell it for half an hour. I'll be right back."

I ran down the street, dodging people as they passed me. By the time I arrived at the restaurant, I was out of breath and had to make myself slow down. The place was really crowded. Just about every seat was taken. It seemed unusual at three in the afternoon, but maybe everyone had been Christmas shopping and had gotten hungry at the same time. My English teacher and my industrial arts teacher were sitting at the counter. I hadn't even known they knew each other. I looked around but I didn't see Joyce. Then Patty walked by, carrying a tray with a pot of tea and some cake on it. "Nina! Let me just put this down. I'll be with you in a minute."

I sat at the back table where the waitresses usually ate. "What a madhouse!" said Patty when she came to sit down. "I've never seen anything like it!" Her face was rosy and her eyes sparkled. I could tell she was actually having a good time. Well, why not? She owned the place.

"I'm looking for Joyce. She's working dinner today, isn't she?"

"I wish she was," said Patty. "We could really use her. But she always says she can get by with just break-

fast and lunch." She peered at my face. "Why? Was
there something you needed?"

I just shrugged. I didn't want Patty to see I was
upset. Where had Joyce been going two nights a week?
I felt sick to my stomach.

"What is it, Nina?" Patty persisted. Suddenly her
kindness seemed overwhelming. I could feel heat come
up into my face and I knew I had to get out of there
before I started to cry.

"I . . . I was going to get some money from Joyce,"
I said. "I saw a Chrismas present I wanted to buy her."

Patty pulled her purse from under the table. "How
much do you need?"

"No, really. I couldn't take anything from you."

"Don't be silly. Your mother can pay me back tomorrow. I promise I won't tell her what it was for."
She gave me a twenty-dollar bill. "Will this be
enough?"

"Sure. Thanks a lot," I said. Then I left the restaurant and bought Joyce the hat. It didn't look so
great to me now, but I bought it anyway.

It was funny. There had been a few other times
Joyce had lied to me, or at least she hadn't been where
she said she was. But I'd never thought of it as lying
before. Even now my mind veered away from that.
Maybe I just hadn't understood her about working
nights.

As I climbed the steps to our apartment, I heard

Silky running across the kitchen floor to meet me. It was late for her walk. "I'm sorry, Silks," I told her. "I'll make it up to you, I promise."

Suddenly I felt like I wanted to go running. Not only wanted to but *had* to. I used to run a lot, especially when we were on the road, but because Joyce wanted me home every day after basketball practice, I hadn't been running in Montpelier. Now with the snow melting would be a perfect time.

I changed into my jogging pants and windbreaker and took Silky outside. Only one or two streets past our block, the town ended and the mountains began. Really, all around us was a vast wilderness. You could see it at night when you drove down the highway. There were just a few clusters of lights to mark the presence of people.

A dirt road went sharply up a hill and I followed it. Soon I was in a forest. I must have run about three miles. I could tell because in the beginning Silky was in front of me chasing after every bird and squirrel, but in the end she was at my side, just trying to keep up with me.

I slowed down to a walk and stretched my arms. I could hear the wind blowing through the pine trees and I saw that it was getting dark. Tears began to slide down my cheeks. What was I doing out here in the woods alone? And where in the world was my mother? I gave in to my feelings and cried harder and harder until I was completely worn out from crying. Then I squatted down by the side of the road and Silky licked my face.

Joyce didn't come home until almost eleven. I was waiting for her in the kitchen, but to make the time pass I'd baked chocolate chip cookies. They were all laid out on aluminum foil, cooling on the kitchen table. I could have eaten some from the first batch, but I had the idea that Joyce and I could have them with tea. As soon as I heard her footsteps on the stairs, I put the kettle on to boil.

"What smells so good?" asked Joyce. Then she saw the cookies. "What a wonderful daughter! You know what? If anyone had given me one wish in the world tonight, I'd wish for chocolate chip cookies."

She could have had as many as she wanted at the restaurant, they made them there, but of course she wasn't *at* the restaurant. For some reason I'd stopped being so upset about that and I had no plans to mention it.

I thought she was probably with a man. When I was coming back home after my run, it had occurred to me. Well, it was only natural. How could she just go on month after month with only me in her life? Joyce is a pretty woman and she has a real sense of style. When I was younger I always had fantasies that she'd meet someone and marry him and then I'd have two parents. But I didn't believe that anymore. Joyce wasn't the type to settle down and get married.

I remember one night when we were living in Seattle. I'd woken up at four-thirty in the morning. We were living in a duplex then and I could hear Joyce crying on the floor below. A man's voice tried to soothe her. I remember exactly what he said: "Don't cry, honey. I promise I'll be gone in the morning." It was true. In the morning there was no sign of him and Joyce never said a word.

Secrets were really common between us. But we were so close we needed our secrets. During this time in Montpelier, Sam Gordon had been mine.

Not that there would have been much to say about him anyway. He and Lynn Cutter had gone around in the halls together for about a week after Jenny Bouchard's party, but then yesterday Lynn had told us at lunch she thought Sam was too stuck up. *I* thought that probably meant he'd broken up with her.

Sam was in seventh grade so he wasn't in any of my classes, but after New Year's the traveling schedule was going to start so I'd see him a lot more. Our two teams would be on buses together going to play other schools. There'd be some night games too and I'd heard what those were like. Sam always said hi now when he saw me. Well, it was better than nothing.

"What are you thinking about?" asked Joyce. She'd taken off her coat and was washing some dishes I'd left in the sink from the chocolate chip cookies. I noticed she was wearing rhinestone earrings and her midnight-blue-and-black checkerboard sweater. It was her favorite outfit at that time.

"Money," I said. Actually I had been thinking about money, but that was about two hours ago.

"Money? How much do you need?"

"No, I already got it. I went to the restaurant and borrowed twenty dollars from Patty. You weren't there." I took the top off the teapot and checked to see if the tea was ready. I couldn't look at Joyce right then.

But she didn't react. She didn't make excuses or try to explain herself. She just sat down and drank some tea and ate five chocolate chip cookies in a row. The word *cool* could have been invented to describe her.

You'd never know I'd as good as caught her lying except maybe for what she did next. She went into the living room and closed the door behind her. "Wait right there. Don't move," she said. "I don't want you to see my hiding place."

I heard rustling sounds and a few minutes later she came back into the kitchen with a small flat package wrapped in Christmas paper. "For you," she said. "An early Christmas present. Because you are my little bunny."

This was a pet name Joyce had for me from when I was very little. She says I had a picture book where a little bunny keeps trying to run away from his mother, but she always finds him and brings him home because he is her little bunny. I guess it means your mother will always love you, no matter what.

"I only have one present so far for you," I told Joyce.

"Don't worry about that. Just open it," she said. She loves giving me presents. She gives great ones too.

I pulled off the wrapping paper and took out a picture in a thin silver frame. It was a watercolor painting, done in miniature, of black and white cows grazing in a meadow. You could see every detail and each of their faces was different. The meadow was green and the sky was red and yellow with purple clouds floating by. In tiny letters underneath the picture, it said *Cows at Sunset*.

"Oh, Joyce. It's beautiful. Thank you."

"I thought you'd like it," she said. "How did I ever guess?"

5 We were having a quiet New Year's Eve, watching a big crowd gather at Times Square on TV, when the phone rang. It was ten at night. Joyce was drinking some scotch and she was so startled it sloshed out of her glass. The phone almost never rings at our house. We only have it in case of emergencies.

I followed Joyce into the kitchen and sat down to

hear what was going on. "Hello," said Joyce. "Who *is* this?" But the call was for me. She handed me the phone.

It was a man's voice and there was a whirring sound in the background, like a fan maybe or a hair dryer. "Nina?"

"Yes."

"It's Mr. Jenks. From school. I'm sorry to call you at home, but I wanted to make sure you come to practice tomorrow. I scheduled an extra one, it's at two o'clock in the gym. I tried you all day but you were out."

It was true. We'd gone shopping in Burlington. One of my Christmas presents had been fifty dollars for clothes, and the stores in Burlington are better than in Montpelier. I'd gotten some really slick stretch pants and a lavender angora sweater, but that's another story.

"I better ask my mother," I said and put my hand over the receiver. "There's an extra practice tomorrow at two. Is it okay if I go? You're working anyway, right?"

Joyce nodded.

"I'll be there," I told Mr. Jenks. I guess he'd called everyone, boys and girls both. Usually the boys' team practiced right after ours. That meant I'd see Sam. I could hang around if I wanted to and watch the boys play, then maybe a bunch of us would wind up going out for pizza. Some kids had already gone a couple of other times, but it was on days when Joyce was home and she wouldn't let me go.

She liked to have me home in the afternoons. Sometimes that made me feel stranded, but at least here we lived in town and I could walk back and forth to basketball practice. In Fairbanks and once before in Cincinnati we'd lived out in the middle of nowhere. It was really boring. After the school bus dropped me off in the afternoon, there had been nothing to look forward to until it came back again in the morning.

When I got off the phone, I went into my own room and opened my closet door. The stretch pants were definitely too fancy to wear tomorrow. I didn't want it to seem like I was planning something. I pulled out a pair of black Levis and tried them on with my new sweater. My hair was growing out from a really short haircut and I held it up on the top of my head and looked at myself in the mirror.

If you want to know, I'm not bad-looking. When I was younger, in third and fourth grade, I used to hate my freckles. But now I think they're all right. I look like lots of other redheaded kids I've known. Pale skin, freckles, wild red hair. And skinny. But actually I've been filling out more lately, catching up to my height, Joyce says.

Sometimes when I'm by myself and feeling confident, I think of Sam Gordon and I think, *How could he not like me?* I smiled and my reflection in the mirror smiled back. I decided that tomorrow at practice I was going to make my move. It was New's Year's Eve, wasn't it? Well, this would be my New Year's resolution.

"I really like Sam Gordon," I said. To Casey Allen and Tammy Emery, as it happens. Now I had no choice because they'd tell everyone about it.

The three of us were in the locker room, getting into our basketball uniforms. They were brand-new and must have come over the vacation. Mr. Jenks had laid them out in a row, in brown paper bags with our names on them, on the bottom bench of the bleachers. Casey and Tammy had been joking about how people wouldn't be able to tell us apart from the boys' team anymore, but when I said that about Sam Gordon, they stopped talking and looked at me.

"I think he's cute. That's all." I was trying to sound like it wasn't that big a deal.

"He might like you too," said Casey. "I saw Lynn Cutter over vacation and she said he liked someone else. She didn't say who."

Even though this was good news, my feelings were hurt. How come Casey had seen Lynn over vacation and she'd never called me? I told myself that they'd probably been friends since they were in kindergarten, probably their parents knew one another—things that had nothing to do with me.

Casey and Tammy and I had changed into our uniforms by now and most of the other kids on the team had arrived. Outside in the gym Mr. Jenks blew his whistle. Practice was beginning.

We ran out onto the gleaming wood floor and kept going around it in laps, four, five, ten times anyway. Mr. Jenks stood by the bleachers with his arms crossed, watching us. Then all of a sudden he began throwing basketballs onto the court, one right after the other. "Form two lines. You, Lewis! Start dribbling. Pass it off to Emery."

I concentrated on the ball motion, trying to keep it smooth. Then I heard Mr. Jenks's whistle. "No, no! Keep your head up! How many times do I have to tell you! Keep looking at that ball and not the other team on Monday, it's going to cost us two points. Okay, Emery. Now it's your turn. Pass it off to Lussier over there."

On Wednesday we were going to play our first game. It was an away game in a town called Newport, way up by the Canadian border. But I hadn't told Joyce anything about it. I don't know what she thought all our practices were for, but I dreaded the moment when I had to tell her I was going to Newport to play a basketball game. She wouldn't like me traveling, I was sure of that.

Mr. Jenks ran us through a lot of other drills and pass patterns. Then the last ten minutes we had a scrimmage. This was always the serious part of practice to me, competing. I was so absorbed in watching for

openings and trying to handle the ball right that everything outside the court disappeared. I didn't think
about Joyce or anyone else. When the buzzer went off
at the end, I was startled to see that most of the boys'
basketball team was sitting in the bleachers watching
us. Sam was there too. Our team had won by four
points and I'd made the last basket. It was a lay-up
that had hit the backboard and then *swish*.

"You want to stay for their practice?" asked Casey.
Maybe she was just being nice, but I thought she might
like someone too. Casey was like me, she didn't usually
say what was on her mind.

We took showers and changed into our clothes and
went back into the gym to watch the boys. Two other
girls came too, Tara Lussier and Julie Ray. It always
amazed me to see how differently the boys played.
Their whole game was so much faster and rougher than
ours. During the scrimmage, Mr. Jenks kept stopping
the clock for personal fouls. For some reason Sam kept
getting fouled, but he made all five of his foul shots.
I loved to see his concentration, the way he rocked
back and forth at the foul line each time before he
shot.

There was no problem about going out for pizza.
One of the boys on the team, Larry Matthews, just
came over to us on his way into the locker room and
invited us. Tara told them we'd go order while they
were changing. Usually it took about a half hour for
Zachary's Pizza to even make the pizzas.

As soon as we got to the restaurant and ordered, all four of us went into the ladies' room to comb our hair. Tara and Julie were already going with players. I wondered who Casey liked.

But when the boys arrived and Sam Gordon slid into the booth next to me, I couldn't think of anything else. This was it. "You played great," I said. Well it was the first thing that came into my mind, and besides he *had* played great.

"You were pretty good too," said Sam. "Where do you live anyway?"

"Kent Street. You know, over by Vermont College?" Our pizza had come, but this conversation was so exciting to me that I had to force myself to pick up a piece and eat it. Hungry was the last thing I was right then. I burned my tongue on the cheese but it didn't matter, I just kept on chewing.

"Wow, this stuff's really hot," said Sam.

"You're telling me! I just burned my tongue on it."

"You did? Let's see."

"You want to see my tongue?" I said. I could feel myself blushing. It has to do with being a redhead, Joyce says—thin skin or something. I'd tried to train myself not to blush. It's awful because it gives you away, but this time I couldn't help it.

"You're blushing," said Sam. He was smiling at me.

I stuck my tongue out at him. What else could I do?

"Uh, Gordon, there are two pieces for you here.

Are you going to eat them or not?" That was Larry
Matthews. He was almost six feet tall.

"Nah, that's okay. You can have them."

Everyone got up to leave. There were pizza crusts
and paper plates and drinking straws all over the table.
It was a real mess. I always felt sorry for the waitresses,
maybe because Joyce was one, so I put everything on
a tray and dumped it into a big garbage can they had.
When I went to get my coat, I saw that Sam had
waited for me.

Outside it was almost dark. There was just a narrow
band of lightness left at the horizon. For a while Sam
and I just walked along and didn't say anything. But
it wasn't like before at Jenny's party, when I thought
he wanted to leave.

"I can't wait till the Newport game," he said just as
we turned onto my street. "We're going to really take
it. No question about it."

"I've never been there. Is it nice?"

"Newport? Who knows? What a weird question."

"I'm just curious, that's all."

"Yeah, maybe that's what I like about you," said
Sam. Right then and there my stomach turned over.
It was a strange feeling. The only thing I can really
compare it to is one time at Great Adventure when I
rode on a roller coaster.

We were at my house. I could see Silky looking for
me out the front window. "That's my dog," I told Sam,
showing him.

"Cute dog. About the game . . . we could sit together on the bus if you want to," he said. I smiled at him and nodded because I could not speak. My stomach had just turned over again.

"Absolutely not," said Joyce. "Forget it."

"What?"

"You heard me. You're not going on a bus to Newport or anywhere else." Joyce wouldn't look at me. She was reading a book and she just kept reading it.

I stood up in the living room. I felt so desperate, I had to move around. What was I going to do? How could I make her let me go? Yet I knew from many other times that when Joyce got like this—when she wouldn't talk to me or look at me—she hardly ever changed her mind.

Usually I'd decide it wasn't worth it anyway. Like once in Pittston, when our whole sixth grade was going to Philadelphia to see the Liberty Bell and the place where the Constitution was written. When Joyce wouldn't sign the permission slip, let's face it, it didn't break my heart.

But the game in Newport was different. To me it seemed as if my whole life and my future were in that trip. If I couldn't go, I'd have nothing. In the first place there was Sam Gordon. I'd been thinking about him every minute, and it was almost like a soap opera on television, waiting to find out what was going to happen next.

But what made me feel *really* awful was our basketball team. We'd learned about a hundred plays and strategies, and since I was center, I was in practically all of them. No one else could play my position. If I couldn't play tomorrow, we'd probably lose, and then nobody on the team would ever talk to me again.

I'd already told Joyce this, but it made no difference to her. "You should have asked me sooner and I would have said no sooner," was what she'd said. "Now it's your problem."

I put on my jacket and mittens and without a word took Silky out for a walk. Snow was falling lightly, drifting down from the sky. I walked around the block and imagined what would happen if Sam were out for a walk too. We would be like Romeo and Juliet in Shakespeare's play, doomed to meet in secret for our love. For some reason this fantasy cheered me up and I began to see my troubles a little more clearly.

I couldn't be too mad at Joyce. Really it was my fault. All along in the back of my mind there had been a doubt about what she'd say when the time came for me to get on a bus and go away to a lot of strange towns. So I'd put off telling her. Other people's mothers would let their daughters go anywhere with anyone and not even think about it, but Joyce and I were different. If she didn't want me traveling all over the state to play basketball, it wasn't to be mean. She just didn't like the idea of the two of us being away from each other and separated by distance. I think it scared her.

It used to scare me too. When I was younger, I had dreams that I was lost in a crowd looking for Joyce everywhere. All the people in these dreams were very menacing, keeping her from me. I can't really describe the sensation; it was a panic so strong that my whole body felt turned inside out. I don't have dreams like that anymore. I think the last one was about two years ago. But I used to wake up from them sobbing and have to be held in Joyce's arms for a long time.

At my feet Silky barked just once. It was like she was saying, "Where are you? Come on, let's go."

A bunch of little kids tumbled out the door of one house carrying their new Christmas sleds. "Have a good time. Don't forget to wear your mittens," called their mother. I started back to my house.

6 It was much worse than I thought it would be. I'd put off quitting basketball until half an hour before the bus was supposed to leave for Newport. A bad idea, I'll admit, but I didn't have the nerve.

The girls' and the boys' teams were both in the gym, sitting in the bleachers and listening to Mr. Jenks's final instructions. Everyone had their bags packed and Sam was in the row of bleachers directly above me. He'd given me a big wave when I came in. I could hardly look at him.

"Are there any questions?"

I raised my hand. My heart was pounding.

"Nina?"

"Could I speak to you for a minute, Mr. Jenks?" I walked onto the gym floor. This felt like the hardest thing I'd ever had to do.

"The rest of you can wait in the parking lot until the bus driver opens his doors." Mr. Jenks must have seen something about my face because he led me back to the bleachers and sat down beside me. "What's wrong, Nina?" he asked.

I started to cry. I couldn't help it. Mr. Jenks is such a huge man, and when he coaches basketball he always seems disapproving and scary, but this time he wasn't scary at all. He handed me his handkerchief and listened to me from start to finish without saying a word.

"Do you think your mother might change her mind?" he asked.

I shook my head. I'd started to cry again, but this time I was sobbing.

"You poor kid," said Mr. Jenks. "One thing I'll tell you right now. None of the other girls on the team are going to take this out on you, I'll make sure of that. I'll have Casey Allen play center up at Newport. She used to come in as center last year sometimes."

"But . . . but . . . I love basketball," I sobbed. It had just occurred to me that this was one more thing I was going to lose.

Mr. Jenks sighed. "I know. And you're a damn good little ball player too. You really use your head out there, which is more than I can say for most of them."

I wish Mr. Jenks had been around the next morning when Jenny Bouchard and Lynn Cutter stopped me on my way to homeroom to say that the Newport team had killed us, 50 to 22. They acted like it was all my fault. "Fred said not to blame you, but what does he expect?" said Jenny.

"Yeah. How come you didn't tell anyone sooner if your mother wouldn't let you play?" asked Lynn. I didn't know what *her* problem was, she was only on the B team, but probably she'd heard about Sam and me.

I shrugged. What was the point of saying anything? I'd been in these situations before, having kids turn against me. I knew it wouldn't change for a while and maybe by the time it did, we'd be gone. I remember something Joyce once said in Cincinnati when I was upset about not getting a part in a play. "We're not talking about Broadway here. It's just some dumb grade school Christmas pageant. Don't let it be important to you and then it won't matter."

I told myself that these girls were just a dumb basketball team and they had no right to be mean to me, but I still didn't feel like facing all of them together at lunchtime. I especially didn't want to see Casey Allen. So I took the three dollars Joyce always gave me and instead of going to the cafeteria, I walked over to the Grand Union and bought myself a hero sandwich from the deli section. We weren't really supposed to do this, but I didn't think I'd get caught. In front of the store was a bench and I sat down and took off my gloves and ate my hero.

Cars kept pulling into the parking lot and women with babies and shopping carts kept coming out of the store. The women all seemed very determined and busy, and I thought of them buying food for their families, how that was their mission in life. Someday I planned to have kids, lots of them to keep each other company, and I would stay in one place and never move, not once.

I heard the twelve-thirty whistle, which always blew at that time from a big machine shop down by the river. I'd have to hurry not to be late to school. But just as I was running up the steps I saw Sam Gordon. He was standing outside but he wasn't wearing a coat. I think he must have been waiting for me in the vestibule. "Nina! I tried to call you last night but your mother said you were sleeping."

It was true. I'd gone to bed really early, at about eight. Joyce knew enough to leave me alone and I hadn't even heard the phone ring.

I didn't know what to say to Sam. Mainly I was

confused. I'd never expected that he'd want to see me now. "Don't you think class is starting? We'd better go." I tried to open the door but Sam blocked my arm.

"What's going on with you, Nina? Mr. Jenks said something about how your mother wouldn't let you play ball?"

"That's it," I said. "That's what's going on."

"But that's ridiculous! Everyone goes out for sports. Why don't you just tell her you're going to do it anyway? She can't stop you, can she?" He sounded really angry.

"That's not the point," I told him. "We have an agreement. If she's worried about me doing something, I don't do it. That's all."

"But what if she's being unreasonable? What if she's trying to stop you from having a normal life?"

"That's only your opinion," I said. I felt like I had to defend myself against him, and yet it was thrilling— the two of us standing on the school steps arguing with each other when any moment a teacher or even the principal could come out.

This Sam Gordon was an amazing boy. He wouldn't take no for an answer either. "I think you have to stand up to your mother. It's not like you're on drugs or something. All we're talking about here is playing basketball. Big deal."

I turned around. The school secretary was coming up the walk smoking a cigarette. When she saw us, she threw it away in the snow. "What are you two doing out here? I believe sixth period started five minutes ago." She stood there and waited until we were both inside and had separated in the hallway to go to our classes.

Joyce had made my favorite dinner, roast chicken with potatoes and carrots. She'd set the table in a special way, too, with candles and one of her flowering plants as a centerpiece. I thought she was trying to make me feel better because of the basketball team, but it turns out she had something else in mind, something really awful.

Looking back, I feel like I should have seen it coming. Our lives did have a pattern and it wasn't the first time. But all I could think about was Sam Gordon. He filled my mind entirely.

Most nights at dinner Joyce and I would tell each other all the things that had gone on that day. I loved to hear Joyce talk about her customers in the restaurant; some of the stories about their characteristics were truly amazing. But that night she seemed nervous and kept jumping up from the table to get things—salt and hot sauce and butter—without saying a word. And since I couldn't exactly tell her about Sam Gordon or cutting school at lunchtime, we ended up eating in silence.

For dessert there was apple crisp with whipped cream that Joyce made at the kitchen counter, standing with her back toward me. Then the second we were through eating, she turned on the overhead light and began clearing the table. "I got a call from Fred Jenks last night. You were sleeping." She'd never even told me about Sam's call, I suddenly realized.

"Mr. Jenks wanted me to let you play basketball with your team. He said you were his best player."

I sat there waiting, suddenly, stupidly, hopeful again. Maybe Mr. Jenks had persuaded her to change her mind.

"Why did you blame it on me?" said Joyce. "Did you tell everyone at school that I was a bad mother?" She faced me with her hands full of place mats and dirty napkins. Under the white fluorescent light, she looked tired more than anything else.

"Of course not."

"You know I can't have you going off every night. I don't do that to you, do I?"

I thought about the Tuesdays and Fridays she was supposed to be working late, but she seemed so upset that I didn't dare say anything.

"I don't like your teachers calling us at home or interfering in our lives. Do you understand? The trouble with this place is that there's nothing to do but play basketball. It's absurd. We need to live somewhere with more going on. A university town maybe like Ann Arbor, Michigan, or Madison, Wisconsin, with concerts and art shows and different events every night. What have we done here? Gone to the movies once or twice and that's it. I don't know why we even got off the highway. We should have just kept on going to Boston."

The more Joyce talked, the more animated she became, pacing around the kitchen and glancing at herself in the little mirror she always hung behind the door. "We'd better hurry if we're going to get you enrolled in another school by second semester. When did you say grades closed here?"

"I don't know."

"Well, find out tomorrow. We'll leave as soon as the marking period is over."

She was ignoring me completely. She wasn't asking my opinion or permission or taking me into account at all. Usually when we moved, it was something we decided together. We'd talk it over and work out when we were leaving and where we wanted to go next. Moving was like a game. Each night we'd put on loud rock and roll and pack until all our boxes were full. Joyce would take care of having the van fixed and I'd make lists of things we should buy for the trip. Finally we'd be sitting in an empty apartment eating pizza and take-out Chinese food on the floor. By the time we left, I'd be glad.

But not now. Even if I couldn't play basketball or have Casey Allen and the other girls like me, I wanted to stay in Montpelier. Of course it had to do with Sam Gordon, I'm not denying it.

It's funny. I'd always thought a girl would be my best friend, and in each place I'd found girls to talk to and do things with. But really I'd see them at school and that was it. When we had to leave, I'd say good-bye and nobody seemed to mind too much. But Sam was different. Aside from the fact that he was boy, he seemed to want—to *really* want—to be my friend. That was the part I couldn't get over.

Joyce had put on a Men at Work tape. I usually liked their music, but it was the wrong choice now. "Can you help me with the bills, Nina? We'll have to close our accounts with the telephone company and the gas and electric, but I'd better pay last month's bills first. Just make a list of how much I owe for each and I'll get the money orders at the bank tomorrow. I've already told Mrs. Brause we're moving."

Mrs. Brause was our landlord. I couldn't believe Joyce had told Mrs. Brause before she'd told me! I followed her into the living room. She was crouched on the floor, going through a cardboard accordion file where she kept our papers.

"You never even asked how I feel about this. What if I don't want to move? What then?" Next to me, Silky pricked up her ears. I was almost yelling but I didn't care.

"We'll move anyway. I shouldn't have to spell it out for you."

"But *why?* Why do we have to move? I really like it here. Another place won't be any better and I'm really doing well in school here. I think I'm going to make the honor roll."

"Please, Nina, don't make this hard on me," said Joyce. She put the accordion file aside and turned off the tape. In the sudden silence we looked at each other angrily. Joyce's arms were clutched in front of her, and her face was pale and smudged with dust. She seemed unhappy, and probably I should have felt sorry for her. But instead I heard Sam Gordon's voice clear as anything. *I think you have to stand up to your mother. . . . What if she's trying to stop you from having a normal life?*

I thought of how it was going to be in a week or two with Joyce and Silky and me in our van full of possessions. Driving along the highway at night while the radio played and trailer trucks passed us going eighty.

A normal life. What was that?

✔ Part Two

Logan, Utah

7   Unless you've driven across it, you have no idea how big this country is. When you stop for meals or stay overnight, a single state can take a whole day, even two. But the Midwest is the worst, the Midwest is endless. Ohio, Michigan, Indiana, Illinois, Wisconsin. With their flat fields, wire fences, and big stormy skies, to me they all looked the same.

We went the long way around, first to Ann Arbor, Michigan, then to Bloomington, Indiana, and then up to Madison, Wisconsin. These towns were university towns and students walked along the wintry streets clutching their books to their chests and talking and laughing.

Joyce was leaving the decision of where we'd live

up to me. I think she might have felt guilty about making us leave Montpelier. The last weeks we lived there were really awful. I decided not to tell anyone at school that we were moving, but Joyce called the office about getting my grades so people found out about it anyway.

Casey Allen and the other girls didn't seem to know how to act with me. They'd been so mean about basketball and now I was leaving. They must have talked about it together, but no one said anything directly or even met my eyes. Still I sat with them at our lunch table up until the last day. What else was I supposed to do?

The only person who was nice was Sam Gordon. I knew he would be. One day my last week we had a half day, and when I left school at noon, Sam was waiting at the gate. Without a word, we began walking together. We went way out of town into the hills where I'd run that time with Silky. Sam had moved twice because of his father's job so we talked about what it was like, how you get used to each place and then the next place seems all wrong. But when I told Sam how many places we'd lived, he stopped walking and just looked at me.

"How can you stand it?" he asked.

"I'm used to it."

"How can you be?" said Sam. "That's crazy." Then he grabbed the branch of a pine tree and shook a lot of snow down on us.

"Hey! What're you doing?" There was snow all over me.

"I'm sorry. I didn't mean it," he said, brushing off my jacket. "Do you ever write letters?"

I nodded even though I never had.

"Write me when you know your address and I'll write you back."

In a way that was what was keeping me going now, the idea of writing Sam. I was already thinking of all the things I could tell him and I was planning to get Joyce to take some pictures of me so I could send them too.

We'd been traveling for eight days and I was sick of it. We'd just about run out of clean clothes and my body hurt from sitting in the van. The roads were icy so I couldn't even go running when we stopped for the night. It wasn't that Ann Arbor and the other towns Joyce wanted to stay in seemed bad. I think I missed the mountains. That was part of it anyway.

So we were heading west. A customer who'd come into the restaurant in Montpelier had told Joyce about a town in Utah that was surrounded on all sides by mountains. It was called Logan and it had a university too. We'd never lived in Utah, but this man also said that things were cheap there and the weather was good. After we left Madison, Joyce asked me what I thought about it. "Sure, I guess. If it has mountains," I said.

By the end of the trip both of us were completely quiet, looking out the window at the scenery passing by. Well, at least there was something to look at. We were driving through a big canyon under a dark gray sky. Then we came into a valley. It must have been twenty or thirty miles long. All around it were mountains covered by snow, but the land in the valley was flat and bare. This was Logan, Utah.

We got to the center of town and Joyce pulled the van into a supermarket parking lot. "We can have dinner in that Pizza Hut and get cleaned up. But take Silky for a walk first."

"Where are we going to stay tonight?"

"In the van," said Joyce. "Where do you think?"

I crossed my arms and didn't move. Joyce was in back rearranging our bags, looking for something, and at first she didn't notice. "Nina, didn't you hear me? I said to take Silky for a walk."

I turned up the car radio until it was blaring. "I want to stay in a motel," I said. I don't know where I was getting my nerve, partly I just wanted to see how far I could push Joyce.

"Is it really important to you?"

"Yes," I answered.

Joyce slid into the front seat next to me and put the van in gear. We cruised the streets of the town and tried a couple of motels until we found one called the Bel-Air. It was cheap enough, Joyce said, so that we could stay for the weekend.

I opened my traveling suitcase and went to take a

shower. Joyce was lying on the bed, just staring at the ceiling. The motel room seemed worn-out and ugly. Instead of feeling like I'd won something, I felt worse than ever.

The rest of that night and all day Saturday Joyce and I didn't really talk to each other. On Saturday we drove around with a real estate agent and looked at about ten houses. They were all tiny, more like bungalows than houses. The one I liked had a round tower with a round room inside. I was not willing right then to say that anything about Logan, Utah, mattered to me one way or the other so I was surprised and happy when we got back to the real estate office and Joyce said we'd rent the tower house.

"Nina can have that room," she told the man as she signed over some traveler's checks. "It's a perfect kid's room."

"They allow dogs, don't they?" I asked.

"Yup, reckon so," the man said. I'd been surprised to hear him talk like a cowboy because he was dressed in a suit and tie.

The next day we moved in and then we did our laundry. I was wondering what to wear to school on Monday and I'd been looking on the streets to see what the styles were like. I couldn't figure out where any people were though. A few cars passed by, but aside from that, everything was quiet. Then in the afternoon, as we were sitting in the Laundromat, we heard a lot of church bells and suddenly there was a traffic jam.

"Mormons," said Joyce. "They're all Mormons."

"What?" I wasn't sure I knew what Mormons were.

"It's a religion. They used to believe in having two or three different wives but I don't think they're allowed to do that anymore. Almost everyone in Utah is a Mormon. Didn't you ever study it in school?"

"I think I would've if we'd stayed in Montpelier. Were they after the Civil War?"

Joyce shrugged. "Probably. Who knows?"

A whole family came in to the Laundromat then, a mother and father and *eight* children. The oldest was about my age and the littlest was a baby. Joyce asked the father something about the dryers and was very polite to him. But the moment we walked out of the place, she shook her head and said, "They don't believe in birth control either."

I knew she meant the Mormons and I wondered what Mormon teenagers would be like. My stomach kind of lurched at the thought. Tomorrow I had to start school. It would be my third school in under a year.

At eight-thirty in the morning Joyce and I were sitting in the Mount Logan Middle School office, waiting for the principal. The school was much quieter and newer than my school in Montpelier and I was glad we'd gotten dressed up. Joyce was wearing stockings, high heels, and the only suit she owned, and I had on my black stretch pants and a red and black Esprit sweater.

"So this is Nina? And she's in the eighth grade?" said the principal after he'd looked over my records. "I see she did very well this year in Vermont, but there's nothing from seventh grade or elementary school."

"They said they'd be sending that," said Joyce.

"Fine. And how did you happen to come to our town, Mrs. Lewis?"

"It was the university."

"Ah," said the principal, looking puzzled. "Do you or your husband work at the university?"

"No, I'm divorced."

"I see," said the principal. He stood up then and took Joyce to the door. She really did look great. She was going job-hunting and would meet me back at our house. It turned out that a school bus stopped right at the corner.

The principal spoke into the PA system and asked someone named Nancy Rudolph to come into the office. "She's the president of the eighth grade," he told me. "She'll take you to your homeroom."

Actually the girl seemed very nice. She was dressed a lot like me and had curly brown hair with red plastic barrettes holding it back. She was a lot shorter than me though.

The halls of the school were empty and very wide.

Here and there along the walls they had full-length mirrors. It was the weirdest thing I'd ever seen. You couldn't help but look at yourself each time you passed one.

"What are those for?" I asked Nancy.

"Self-esteem. They put them up to make people feel proud of themselves."

"It seems strange for school, kind of distracting."

"I guess!" said Nancy. "But you should see, the boys are the ones who really stare at themselves. They comb their hair for hours."

This girl was so easy to talk to! I felt like we were going to be friends for sure. She seemed young for her age but she didn't make me nervous like the girls in Montpelier. When we got to homeroom, she asked the teacher if I could sit next to her, and she walked with me to all our classes.

The teachers seemed pretty serious about teaching here, but the work wasn't hard for me. They took you through it step by step. Aside from Mr. Callahan, who taught English and liked to crack jokes about his wife and family, they were much stricter than my teachers in Montpelier.

When I looked around at the kids, it was the most surprising thing though. Most of the girls, I'd say ninety percent of them, reminded me of Nancy Rudolph. They were dressed like her (and me) in stretch pants or baggies and cotton sweaters. They didn't wear any makeup, and when Nancy introduced me to some of her friends at lunchtime and in the halls between classes, they were all really friendly and welcoming.

The boys were sort of the same. They didn't wear fancy clothes or anything, and they seemed kind of young, even younger than the girls. I didn't see anyone with the good looks and coolness of Sam Gordon, that was for sure.

But in each of my classes there were two or three kids who were *totally* different. These kids seemed more like high school kids than eighth graders. They didn't look exactly punk. Tough is more like it. The girls had on skintight jeans and wore high heels and tons of makeup. One girl's eyeliner went all the way into her hair on each side. The boys wore tight jeans too and had their hair slicked back with gel. I noticed they all had on heavy black boots instead of sneakers.

I'd never seen kids my age who looked like this in any of my other schools, and it seemed really surprising in Logan where everyone was so fresh and clean-cut.

"Who are those kids?" I asked Nancy Rudolph at lunch. They were all sitting together in two tables way at the back of the cafeteria. In this school the cafeteria was a big room with lots of windows. The food was free and it was good too, much better than in Montpelier.

"Which kids?"

"In the back over there."

Nancy looked around. "Oh, them. They're rockers."

One of her friends, a girl named Doris Baker, said,

"We stay away from them. They drink and smoke cigarettes. Their parents are divorced and they're always getting in trouble."

Damn! Why had Joyce told the principal that she was divorced? I hoped it wouldn't get around the school, the way things did in Montpelier. I was already planning to tell everyone my father had died. In an accident maybe, when I was too little to remember him.

I was really tired by the end of school from having to learn so many new names and people, but I had to admit it was a good first day. Nancy and Doris and another friend of theirs named Laureen even invited me to go shopping with them at a mall. "It's got a J.C. Penney's and a Luv's," said Doris. "Did you have those in Vermont?"

"Not a Luv's but a Penney's. They're all over the place, nationwide."

The last bell rang and Nancy took my arm. "It'll be really fun. Call your mother and tell her my mother will take you home later."

"I can't. She's expecting me on the bus. Anyway we don't have a phone yet."

All of which was true. But I already realized we lived way across town and Joyce would probably want me home on the bus every afternoon like she had in Fairbanks. I didn't think I could stand being that lonely again.

Outside the sun was hot and bright. Spring didn't seem so far away. I thought about riding bikes on the flat streets or sunbathing with a group of girls in someone's backyard. The kids here were really interested in me and I wanted to see them more than just at school. Joyce or no Joyce, I'd have to manage it somehow.

8

The school bus was brand-new. It didn't rattle as it went down the roads, and the ride was even kind of lulling since the bus driver was playing easy-listening music on the radio. I didn't pay much attention to who else was on the bus since I was looking out the window, trying to see how to get to my house from school. All the streets were named for directions and numbers. 300 North, 100 West, 900 South. It would be pretty hard to get lost.

But the last time the bus stopped, there were only three of us left—me and two boys who were wearing identical black leather jackets. Rockers for sure. I wondered if they were our neighbors, but they walked in the other direction from me.

When I came into the house, Silky came bounding over, sliding across the linoleum floor in the entryway. All the other rooms in this house were carpeted, even the bathroom and kitchen. Joyce was standing by the kitchen sink, unwrapping some house plants she must have just bought.

"Look, aren't these pretty?" she said, holding one up. "I couldn't resist. Why not, I figured, we can afford it. My new job starts tomorrow. You wouldn't have believed it, Nina, I could have had my pick of five jobs. And everything is so cheap here."

"What is it?" I asked.

"My job?"

I nodded. What did she think I meant?

"I'm going to work in a newspaper office. It's the only newspaper in town and they need someone to check the AP reports when they come off the scanner, which they do all night long."

"Why did you take a night job?" I was trying to figure out if that would give me more freedom or less.

"It paid the best. But don't worry, you'll already be asleep when I leave, and in the mornings you can get your own breakfast and catch the bus. The hours are from midnight to eight."

"But what if I want to stay after school sometimes and do things with my friends? Will you be able to pick me up?"

"That depends," said Joyce. "We'll see."

Not what you'd call an enthusiastic response, but there was no point in pushing it right now or making a scene. I remembered something Joyce told me her mother used to say. "You can catch more flies with molasses than you can with vinegar." It meant you could get more by being nice to someone than by being mean.

Our kitchen stuff was still in boxes, wrapped in newspaper, so I started going through everything, putting it away. At the same time Joyce went out to the van and carried in about four bags of groceries. "I thought we'd have Mexican food for supper. They have lots of Mexican specialties in the supermarket. I guess Mexico's not too far from here."

"Closer than Vermont anyway."

"Right," said Joyce. She turned on the radio and the five o'clock news came on. They were talking about the price of hogs and oil rights in Utah. We began fixing supper. In a way I felt companionable with Joyce, as though nothing had changed between us. And yet when I thought about Montpelier, it still really hurt me.

"Cut these onions, Nina, and I'll do the tomatoes and lettuce for the tortillas."

I blamed what happened on the knife. It was my fault. I had just sharpened all our knives. This one had a narrow steel blade, and when it slipped, it opened up the flesh of my left thumb with surprising neatness and speed. Only the blood draining from the wound made me realize what happened. The onions on the chopping block were soaked with blood.

"Jesus Christ, Nina! What have you done to yourself?" Joyce grabbed my hand and thrust it into the sink, turning on the water. My thumb began to throb and I could see that the cut was deep. At the bottom there was something different than flesh, something hard and white as if I had hit a bone.

"Hold it up high in the air. Here, wrap this around it. Keep it above your heart." Joyce handed me a roll of paper towels and ran out of the room. I knew from experience she was going to get her first-aid kit.

Joyce carried an amazing amount of supplies around with us and she always knew exactly what to do in an emergency. Once when we were crossing Oregon, I twisted my ankle in a woodchuck hole. It swelled way up and hurt like crazy. The doctor thought he should do an X ray, but Joyce refused and said it was only a sprain. I had to hop on one foot, and I can still remember the shock on the man's face when she told him we were leaving. She was right though—my ankle healed fine on its own.

"You've really done it this time, kiddo," she told me. "I think you're going to need stitches." She led me over to the kitchen table and unwrapped my thumb. It was still bleeding, but at a slower rate. She poured some kind of disinfectant over it and I didn't even scream.

"I want you to squeeze the two sides of the cut together like this. Squeeze them as hard as you can."

I could not believe it! She had taken out a needle and thread and *she was stitching up my thumb!* I closed my eyes and felt my head explode with pain. How could my own mother be doing this to me? Weren't there painkillers that would make it not hurt? I don't know how many times the needle went through my skin, but when I opened my eyes, three stitches were in my thumb.

"There. That wasn't as bad as it could have been. You should see yourself, Nina. You're white as a ghost." She took her bottle of scotch from under the kitchen sink and made me have some in a glass. The taste was awful and it burned my mouth. "Have some more," Joyce said.

An hour later my hand hurt more than ever, but I was halfway drunk, I think, and lying on my mattress with a cold washcloth on my forehead. Around me the windows of the tower room looked out into the darkness.

God, what a weird thing to have happened! I guess Joyce knew what she was doing, but I wished she'd taken me to a doctor. "We just got here. I don't even know how to get to the hospital, much less the name of a doctor," was all she'd say. To me that didn't make sense, and I thought there was probably something about doctors in general that scared her. She didn't trust them, that was for sure.

When I woke up the next morning, the house was quiet. Next to my mattress were a bowl of cereal, a glass of milk, and an apple. Propped up next to the cereal was a note. "I hope your thumb is feeling much

better. Take two Tylenol for pain. See you at 4:00.
Love, Mom."

My whole hand was stiff and sore but the gauze on
the cut had no blood on it. I guess that meant it was
healing all right. Still, I was sure the kids at school
would ask me what happened. Just what I needed
. . . another strange thing about myself to have to
explain.

But actually when I got in to my homeroom, everyone was very sympathetic. When I said I had stitches,
they didn't even ask where I'd gotten them. Instead
Doris Baker showed me a big scar on her wrist with
five stitches. "I put my hand through a window. I
couldn't even see it. My mother had just washed all
the windows in the house."

"I never had stitches," said Nancy Rudolph.

"You're lucky," Doris said.

Today after school these girls were planning to go
bike-riding. There was one place east of town that all
the kids gathered in. I think it was a sand pit. The
older boys raced motorcycles there and the kids my
age took their bicycles and did tricks, pop-up wheelies
and things.

Bike-riding was really big in Logan. Everyone had
freestyle bikes. I'd already seen them parked in a long
row in the school parking lot, and at recess Nancy and
Doris and another girl named Janis Mitchell took me
outside and showed me which ones were theirs.

"What's your bike like?" Doris asked.

"It's a ten-speed." Joyce and I both had ten-speeds. They were good because they were lightweight and the front wheels came off for packing. But we hadn't used them in Vermont because the hills were too steep. Joyce was always talking about how she had to get in shape, but she never did much about it.

"Maybe your parents would let you trade it for a freestyle bike," said Janis. "You should go to Lindsay's Bike Mart. They're not that expensive there."

The bell rang for the end of recess. I decided now was the time to say something about my father. "Actually it's just my mother and I. My father died when I was a year old. I don't even remember him."

I saw the girls' faces change, with surprise and some kind of greedy curiosity registering at the same time. It was a look I'd seen before. I knew they wanted to find out just how my father died, but they would never ask.

"He was a tractor-trailer driver," I said. "His rig jackknifed in a rainstorm." I'd heard a waitress in a diner say this once and for some reason it had stuck with me.

I'd seen plenty of big trucks on the highways, but I really didn't know anything about them. Joyce had warned me all my life not to talk to truck drivers in the places we stopped at. It was too bad in a way—they were always the friendliest people we met on the road, and especially when I was little they'd try to get my attention. I used to be scared they were going to capture me and take me with them. But now I think they were just men far away from home who missed their wives and children.

Nancy and the other girls were looking at me strangely. They must have asked me a question. "Nancy just wanted to know if you were coming with us after school," said Doris. "My house is only two blocks away and my younger brother has a bike you could borrow."

"I can't today because of my hand. My mother's going to take me to the doctor. But tomorrow I'll come for sure."

My heart was sinking even while I said this. I didn't want to start lying to people, it was a bad practice to get into. Actually when we lived in Fairbanks, I'd found myself telling lies all the time. In that town I said I had a father and even a cute little brother, but I never made any close friends and we lived so far from school that I was never caught. Still it made me really nervous, and I was proud that in Montpelier I hadn't told a single lie. I vowed this was going to be my last one in Logan too.

On the bus going home, the same two boys were there. I said hi just to be friendly and also because I wanted to see what they'd do. One of them, the bigger one, raised his chin to acknowledge me, but that was it. He was actually kind of handsome, or at least unusual-looking, with a narrow face and straight black hair. I wished I could see his eyes, but he was wearing mirrored sunglasses.

These rockers interested me. I certainly wasn't afraid of them like Nancy and her friends were. Are you kidding? There I was on the bus, having to get up my nerve just to ask Joyce if I could see kids my own age. Next to Joyce, rockers were nothing.

It was a beautiful day, with a hot sun beating down. When I came to our house, Joyce and Silky were outside on the front steps. Joyce was knitting and Silky was just sitting there, wagging her tail.

"This is really the life, kiddo. Have you ever seen such great weather? The air's so clear, it hurts your eyeballs."

"Hi, Joyce." I bent down to give her a kiss. "Can you take me to the doctor this afternoon? I think someone should look at my cut."

"Has it been bothering you?" asked Joyce.

"No, but still . . ."

"I'll take a look at it later. You know what? You never told me about school yesterday."

This was it. I *had* to ask Joyce if I could go bike-riding with Nancy and Doris. I couldn't keep putting them off day after day. I buried my hands in Silky's hot coat and started in. "School's okay. The work is pretty easy. But you should see, Joyce. The girls in my class are *so* friendly to me. Everyday they've asked me to do something with them. Tomorrow we're supposed to go bicycle riding together."

"We are?" said Joyce ominously, getting to her feet.

"I told them I could come. I didn't think you'd mind. One of the girls promised to lend me a bike. They all have freestyle bikes out here. Probably her mother could bring me home if you can't pick me up. I'd be home in time to help with supper."

I knew I was talking too much but I couldn't seem to stop, not with Joyce standing three steps above me with her hand on the front door and her face so angry.

"I thought we'd already been through this in Montpelier," she said.

"Through what?"

"Nina, think about it. How many times do you need to be told? You have no right agreeing to do anything with anyone without asking me first."

"But it's only bike-riding. I promise I'll be back before dark."

"No. The answer's no."

At that moment some sense I'd always had of Joyce suddenly shifted over. I was looking right at her and I realized I didn't care anymore if she was angry or not. Too bad for her! I was mad too!

Our bicycles were parked next to the van, leaning on their kickstands. I rushed over and grabbed mine and headed down the street in the direction of the snowy mountains. "Come back here!" Joyce yelled after me.

"Why should I?" I yelled.

Silky followed me, barking, but I pedaled like crazy until she finally turned back. The paved road gave way to dirt and soon the little houses were far behind me. Out here there were only farms. I wanted to be alone but I also wanted to pay Joyce back and make her see that she couldn't run my life.

This was still in February before daylight savings time. I must have ridden for about an hour and I sat down on a cement bridge over a culvert and watched some brown-and-white cows who were standing nearby. It was beginning to get dark and the cut on my thumb was hurting. A car came up behind me, the first one in a long time, and I knew before I even looked that it would be Joyce.

"Get in here," she said. "What kind of fool are you?"

"What's going to happen?" I asked. I didn't feel like talking about it. I knew I was in trouble and I wanted to know what it would be.

"You're grounded. I want you home every day right after school. No bike-riding, no running, you can't even walk Silky around the block."

"For how long?" I asked.

"A month. And don't think I'm happy about it either. But if you're going to act like a brat, I'm going to have to treat you like one."

This kind of fighting was completely unlike Joyce and me. She'd never even punished me before. My reaction to it was weird though. When we got in the van and were driving back into town, I felt calm and almost contented. Well, I thought, if this is the worst she can do to me, I have nothing to be afraid of.

9

March 22

Dear Sam,

Hi, sorry I haven't written before. I hope you're not mad at me.

How's everything in Montpelier? How is the girls' basketball team doing? I hope they are winning some games. What about the boys' team? Are you high scorer?

My mother and I are living in Logan, Utah. (If you want, you can look on a map.) It's a pretty cool place, but no one cares about sports at all. They only play basketball in gym class. The towns in Utah are so far apart they'd probably have to drive all day to play another team. I've been working on my shot though. We have a basketball hoop in our driveway.

I've made some really neat friends here and every day we go bike-riding after school. I told my one friend Nancy about you and she wanted to see what you look like. Sooooo . . . can you send a picture of yourself? I wanted to send one of me but our camera is broken right now.

At my new school they have this weird custom, they celebrate birthdays by having the girl's close friends come over to her house and wake her up. She's not allowed to get dressed or brush her hair or anything. She has to go around all day in her pajamas and bathrobe, even in school. Can you believe it? Her parents take everyone out to breakfast at McDonald's before school starts.

I've already been to one of these parties and next week it's Nancy's birthday so we're having one for her. Three girls plus me are coming. I can hardly wait!!!

Well, I better go now. I have to do my social studies homework. Tell Mr. Jenks I said hi, but don't tell anyone else.

Bye. Write soon.

Love,
Nina

The last part of that letter was absolutely true. We *were* having a breakfast party for Nancy and I *was* going. I'd been planning it for about two weeks. Since Joyce didn't get home from work until after I was in school, she'd never know where I'd been. All I had to do, I figured, was set the alarm for five-thirty and walk over to Nancy's house. She lived pretty far away but I'd walk fast. It should take me no more than an hour. I even had a present for Nancy, a wide pink cinch belt that Joyce had given me for Valentine's Day but I'd never worn.

In a way it was amazing to me that I'd even been invited to Nancy's party. After Joyce grounded me, I expected Nancy and Doris and their other friends to lose all respect for me. I told them the next day what had happened, that I'd been grounded for a month, but instead of ruining my chances, it seemed to make me even more interesting in their eyes.

"You're so funny," Nancy told me. "Why did you think we'd mind? My mother is strict too, but I have to admit, a month is a little long. Are you LDS?"

I shook my head. I already knew that LDS stood for Latter-Day Saints, which was another name for Mormons.

"I didn't think so," said Nancy. "Laureen's Catholic. Her parents make her go to mass almost every morning. Haven't you noticed how she's always falling asleep in homeroom?"

"I am not!" said Laureen. "You're not even *in* my homeroom.

"Well, that's what Janis told me." Nancy put on some lip gloss and immediately blotted it off. We were in the girls' room, getting ready to go outside. Even though none of these girls actually wore makeup, I think they wished they did.

Every day at school we had twenty minutes after lunch to do whatever we wanted. Our group always hung out on top of a tall metal stairway leading to the school yard. It was away from everyone else and it gave us a great view of the boys where they were playing baseball.

But we did more than just watch them. Yesterday we'd started a list, rating each boy according to his attributes. For example, Donny Michaelson had a good body, fair face, good personality, good clothes, excellent athletic ability. Kurt Moger had an excellent body, excellent face, bad personality, excellent clothes, fair athletic ability. Even though I didn't really know anyone, I could still comment on their looks. So far, we'd only rated six or eight boys who were the most popular in our class, but we planned to go through everybody.

The one boy I kept coming back to in my thoughts was the rocker from my bus, so finally I decided to ask about him. I could see him on the playground, but he wasn't playing baseball with the boys below us, he was leaning on the fence with three other rockers, one boy and two girls.

The funny thing was that even though my friends talked about boys all day long, they really didn't go out with anyone. There were no boy-girl parties in Logan and only the rockers held hands in the halls or walked with their arms around each other. On the whole playground they were the only group that was integrated, boys and girls.

"See that rocker over there. Do you know his name?" I asked.

"Which one?" said Doris.

I didn't mean to point. "The one with the mirrored sunglasses. The tall one."

"Oh, that's Daryl Carpenter," Laureen said. "I think he's supposed to be a freshman but he was kept back."

"Let's put him on the list."

"You're not serious!" said Doris.

"Why not? We said we were going to do everyone."

"That's right," Nancy put in. "If Nina wants him on the list, he should definitely be on it." She was the one doing the writing, but all of us crowded over to the stairway railing to get a better look at Daryl.

"Well, he's not bad-looking," said Laureen. "But why does he have to wear those weird glasses? You can't even see his eyes."

"That's the point, you jerk," said Doris.

There was a lot of discussion back and forth but in the end here's how we rated him: *Daryl Carpenter*. Body, excellent. Looks, good. Personality, ? Clothes, poor. Athletic ability, ? I was satisfied, even though if it were up to me, I would have rated his clothes better. I've always admired leather jackets, ever since I saw the movie *Top Gun*.

That afternoon on our bus Daryl sat down in the seat right in front of me. For once he was by himself, and because of our list I felt as though someone had introduced us to each other and we were already friends. Now that's really weird! All I could see was the back of his head but it was so familiar to me. I had to stop myself from reaching out and ruffling his hair.

But after everyone else got off the bus and we were almost at our stop, he suddenly slid in next to me. It was such a shock! I didn't say a word but my heart started beating a mile a minute and I could feel my face flush.

"Why were you and your friends looking at me at lunchtime today? What were you saying about me?" His voice was deeper than a boy's voice and it had a funny flat twang. When I looked at him, I saw my reflection in his sunglasses.

"You're Daryl Carpenter, right? I was just asking them who you were, that's all."

"You should have asked me," he said.

"Yeah, sure. Your friend is always with you and you never even say hello to me." Where was I getting my braveness? I had no idea.

"That's not my friend, he's my brother. He stayed home sick today."

"Oh, I hope he's okay."

Daryl gave me a look like I was crazy. The bus driver pulled the bus to a stop and swung open the doors for

us. "What do you care?" said Daryl. "You don't even
know him."

I didn't know whether to apologize or what. But as
soon as he got out, he walked away from me without
another word. I was so excited I felt like clapping. I
tried to hold on to that feeling as I walked up the
street to my house.

It was hard being home since Joyce had grounded
me—everything had gotten really strained and un-
natural between us. She was waiting for me now in
the living room, reading a magazine and trying to act
cheerful. "How was school today?" she asked, the same
way she did every afternoon.

"Fine," I said. And that was all. I called Silky over,
then I got myself some cookies and milk and went into
my room. It wasn't that I wanted to be mean to Joyce.
I just had nothing to say to her. As far as I was concerned, she was a million light-years away from me.
We were like two planets, each spinning in our separate orbits.

My tower room in Logan was by far the best room
I'd ever had. For the first time in years I hadn't put
up my sunset collage. There was no need to, since four
windows in the room faced west and you could see the
real sun actually setting over the mountains. The white
snow would reflect all the colors in the sky. It was an
amazing sight. I'd go into my room every afternoon
and wait for it, lying on my bed and listening to music
on my Walkman.

I think I was probably better than most kids my age at being alone doing nothing. All the days and weeks and months of driving had given me plenty of experience, and the world inside my own head seemed perfectly full and rich to me. I loved to wander around in there, thinking my thoughts and dreaming my dreams. Today for the first time they were about Daryl Carpenter. I felt disloyal, but I couldn't help it. The image of him had just totally eclipsed Sam Gordon's. It was as if I were seeing Sam far away from an enormous distance while Daryl was right in front of me, up close.

Looking through my tapes, I chose one by Bruce Springsteen, *Born in the U.S.A.* Every word of every song could have been about Daryl. And when I listened to the more romantic songs like "Dancing in the Dark" and "Cover Me," I knew I was a goner.

A couple of hours later when the sunset had faded to just a purple glow, Joyce suddenly appeared in my room. I hadn't heard her come in, but of course I was still listening to my Walkman. I took the headphones off my ears. I didn't want to be blatantly rude.

"Supper's ready." Joyce picked up the sweater I'd worn that day and draped it over my closet door. "Why is your room such a mess lately? You always used to be so neat."

I shrugged. I really didn't think there was an answer to that question. Or else I could have said, *It's my room, it's my life, no one asked you to come in here,* but my punishment was supposed to end next weekend and I wasn't going to endanger that in any way.

When I came into the kitchen, the table was already set and the food was on our plates. I never helped with the cooking anymore. I never offered and Joyce didn't insist. Tonight we were having macaroni and cheese, but by the time we sat down, it was stone-cold.

"You know, there's supposed to be this huge lake only about thirty miles from here," said Joyce. "Bear Lake, I think it's called."

"I've heard of it."

"Yes, well . . . I was thinking we might want to take a ride up there sometime."

I shrugged. "Maybe," I said.

It was almost as though Joyce had been grounded along with me. All she ever did lately was stay home. She hadn't said much about the people at the newspaper, but I knew she was the only woman on the night shift and probably she hadn't made any friends there. It was her problem, I told myself. If she wanted me to keep her company and take car trips with her up into the mountains, then she should be more understanding and let me do things with my own friends sometimes.

When I stood up and cleared my plate from the table, Joyce said, "You hardly ate any supper."

"I guess I wasn't hungry," I said. Then I went up to my room to do my homework, closing the door behind me.

10 I woke up and looked at the green glowing numbers on my alarm clock. It was four-thirty in the morning. No wonder it was still dark.

Today was Nancy's breakfast party and I'd been so worried about getting up on time that I really hadn't slept all night. All around me the house felt silent and spooky and empty. "Silky, Silky," I whispered, and was relieved to hear her yawn and stretch somewhere in my room. I knew the doors were locked and I was safe here alone, but still . . .

Part of my nervousness, I think, came from having to sneak around to go to Nancy's party. I'm not one of those kids who easily breaks rules. I wasn't used to them because Joyce had never really given me any rules before. "You're so grown-up for your age, Nina. I'll just expect you home on time," she'd say. Sometimes it was still hard for me to believe how things had changed between us.

I lay in bed awhile, feeling my mind dart around in a hundred different directions. Then I realized I'd never fall back to sleep, so I got up and turned on my light. I'd planned to get up soon anyway.

I got dressed slowly and took a tour around to make sure everything looked as though I'd left the house at the regular time. Then I put my present for Nancy into my schoolbag and stepped out through the door.

The sky was cloudy and it was beginning to get light. There wasn't a soul in sight. I walked through our neighborhood and studied all the little houses to see if I could find any signs that Daryl might live in one. I don't know what I was looking for, his name on the mailbox maybe or a motorcycle parked out front. I wasn't sure he had a motorcycle, I just imagined that he might.

We'd had one other conversation since our first one. I'd asked him how his brother was feeling and Daryl said his father had taken him to the doctor that day. His brother was in sixth grade and his name was Joel. I liked to think Daryl was worried about his brother but trying not to show it.

In that conversation he'd been much friendlier to me. And even though I couldn't fit it in with the rest of my life in Logan, I still imagined us walking around town, holding hands and telling our secrets to each other. I wondered if he had a mother or why his father had been the one to take Joel to the doctor. Maybe his family was weird in some way too.

My trip to Nancy's house took me through the center of town and right past the Mormon temple. You couldn't possibly miss this structure. It was about five stories taller than any other building in Logan and it stood by itself high on a hill. Other churches had one spire, but the temple had two. I'm not sure why.

In over a half hour of walking, I hadn't seen anyone at all, but now the street was filled with people. There were, I'd say, close to fifty people milling around, carrying small suitcases and valises, and calling greetings to each other in the still air. Cars and even buses were double-parked in front of the temple and the whole place looked like a giant terminal with passengers coming and going. This was really something! I'd have to ask Nancy just what these Mormons were doing at six-thirty in the morning.

Her house was on a street that looked a lot like ours. It had the same small houses with big yards set back from the sidewalk, but I was surprised to see three sheep grazing on her lawn. Some people in Logan kept farm animals, but I didn't know Nancy's family did. She hadn't mentioned it.

I checked my watch as I came up her front walk. I was exactly on time. Her mother opened the door before I even knocked, putting her finger on her lips to let me know I should be quiet. In the living room four little kids, two boys and two girls, were sitting on the couch. I guessed they were Nancy's brothers and sisters, though nobody said a word.

A few minutes later Janis, Laureen, and Doris arrived together and we all tiptoed up the stairs to Nancy's room. She must have shared it with her sisters because there were two other beds, but what amazed me was that the beds were already made. The bedspreads and the pillowcases had a Strawberry Shortcake theme and the walls of the room were bright pink. I was glad I'd brought a pink cinch belt for Nancy. I hadn't been sure if she'd like something so feminine.

Yesterday at school we'd decided to wake her up by singing "Happy Birthday to You," but before we could begin, Nancy's mother surprised everyone by passing around kazoos. Kazoos are little metal instruments sort of like whistles. She showed us how to hold them in our mouths and whispered that we should just sing through them. The tune sounded like "Happy Birthday" all right, but the words were louder and they hummed and vibrated. When Nancy woke up, she looked really panicked, like *What's going on here? Where am I? Is this outer space, or what?*

We all cracked up and then Nancy got out of bed and she laughed too. "Do I really have to wear my pajamas? Can't I just brush my teeth?" she asked, but really she knew the rules for breakfast parties.

Her little brothers and sisters were gone by the time we went downstairs, and we all piled into their car, a big rattly station wagon. Well, they needed it for that family. Outside a light rain had started falling. I was sitting in the front seat between Nancy and her mother and I felt entirely happy and as if everyone there liked me. The word *carefree* came into my mind. *Free of cares.*

The McDonald's in Logan was like every other McDonald's I'd ever been to. It even smelled the same, like moist hamburger buns. Someone once told me that they had a special spray they used to make that smell, but I found it hard to believe. Why bother?

We sat down at two tables next to each other and Nancy and her mother went up to the counter to get our breakfasts. We'd all decided to have Egg Mc-Muffins, hot chocolate, and orange juice. I thought Nancy was brave to walk across the crowded restaurant dressed in her pajamas, but either people didn't notice or they were just being polite by not staring at her. At this hour it was mainly adults on their way to work. A lot of people were lined up to take food out. Probably they were going to eat at their desks.

We'd just gotten our food when I happened to look outside through the plate-glass window. Two men and a woman were getting out of a car. The woman's head was turned toward one of the men and he had his hand on her waist. Then she looked up and I saw that it was Joyce.

I felt as if I'd been socked in the stomach. Suddenly all the sounds in the restaurant vanished. My friends were talking and laughing but I could not hear them. Suspecting nothing, they were unwrapping their sandwiches and sipping their hot chocolate. Joyce and the men stood at the counter only ten feet away.

I sat there and waited, staring at my food. Irrelevantly it occured to me that I'd had nothing to eat since last night. Nancy had put all her presents in a pile on the table. Right on top was the cinch belt that I'd given her, the cinch belt Joyce had given me. This was really a nightmare.

Now Joyce was walking over to our table. I could

see her stockinged legs approaching, scissoring back and forth. "Hello, everyone," she said. "I'm Nina's mother."

I looked up then and saw not so much Joyce as the two men who'd come in with her. They were both wearing white shirts and ties, but the ties were loose at their throats and their shirt sleeves were rolled up. At this moment I couldn't recall which one had been touching Joyce.

"Would you like to sit down, Mrs. Lewis?" said Nancy. "Did Nina tell you that we were coming to McDonald's?"

"Oh, yes. She told me everything." Joyce's smile was so false, it was frightening. But of course no one but me knew what her real smile looked like. "I'd like to borrow Nina for just a minute, if I may," she said.

We went past the table where the two men were eating. They had huge breakfasts, it would take them a long time to finish. "My daughter, Nina," said Joyce. Let's get this over with, I thought.

But as soon as we were outside, she grabbed me by the shoulders and began shaking me back and forth, over and over again. "Do you know how angry I am? Do you? Do you?" she screamed.

It was like the two of us were locked in some kind of crazy dance in the parking lot of McDonald's. I stood there in full view of my friends with my head wobbling on my neck, and cars and people skipping around in my field of vision, hating her with all my might. "There! Have you had enough now?" she screamed.

From inside the restaurant the two men had somehow appeared and they came up to Joyce and led her over to their car. "Go on back inside," one of them said to me before they drove away. I saw Joyce's scared face behind the windshield for a moment and I began to cry.

My friends were all pressed up against the window, watching. But when I looked at them, they went and sat down as if nothing had happened. Nancy beckoned to me. The idea of explaining or even going inside seemed impossible. But I certainly wasn't going home.

I sat down on a bench next to the restaurant and waited, trying to calm down. After a while, Nancy's mother came out, carrying a white paper bag. "Your breakfast was getting cold, so we got you this to eat in the car on the way to school. Are you all right?" she added.

I nodded, grateful for her kindness. Nancy was always kind too. I realized then that no one was going to force me to explain anything or even refer to what had happened. But it didn't matter. Now these girls had terrible evidence, proof that my life was not normal, not like theirs at all. And even though they might be kind, in that moment, as the car splashed through the shiny, rainy streets and all five of us sat with our hands in our laps, saying nothing, I made up my mind that I could not be friends with any of them again. I was too ashamed.

In the afternoon when I got out of school, our van was parked outside near all the waiting buses. I can't say I was surprised. As I walked over to it, Joyce leaned across the front seat and opened the door on the passenger side. "I'm sorry," she said before I even got in. "I never should have lost control of myself that way."

"That's okay. It was me who broke my punishment."

All day at school I'd been thinking about Joyce. I felt a real coldness in my heart when I remembered her hands on me, but I'd decided I had to get along with her. I wasn't going to run away and live on the streets of Salt Lake City, that was for sure. And I didn't want any more fights or punishments right now when my life was changing so fast.

Today after lunch I'd spent time with Daryl Carpenter. It was easy. I kept thinking of how I couldn't have my friends now anyway, then I just walked up to Daryl on the playground where he was standing with two girl rockers and said, "Hi. How're you?"

He seemed surprised to see me and looked around, craning his neck in an exaggerated way. "Where are Nancy Rudolph and Doris? I don't think I recognize you alone."

"Don't be silly," I said. "You see me alone all the

time." The two girl rockers were watching me and they didn't seem very friendly, but I wasn't going to let that bother me. "Do you want to walk around in front of school?" I said.

With Daryl I had the feeling I could do anything I wanted and it wouldn't matter. That might sound conceited, but really it was just the opposite.

He stood back and took a good look at me. I held my breath and waited for him to decide my fate. I was glad I'd worn nice clothes because of Nancy's party. "Sure, why not?" he said at last.

It wasn't like anything special happened on our walk. The grass was wet from the rain and we couldn't go far. But a lot of people saw us together and that was what really mattered. That, and the last thing he'd said to me: "You're really pretty, even if you do look about ten years old."

As Joyce and I rode home in the van, I opened the glove compartment to see if my makeup case was still in it. When we were traveling, one of the things I did to make the time pass was to practice putting makeup on. Good, it was in there and nothing had spilled or melted.

From now on I planned to wear makeup to school in Logan. I'd always worn it in Montpelier anyway. I wouldn't have to put on ugly black lines or heavy foundation like the girls with Daryl. I was much more skillful than that. Just some violet eye shadow to bring out my eyes, and blusher for my cheekbones and across my forehead, the way Joyce had shown me. At least it would make me look older.

As we were coming up to our street, she slowed way down as if she wanted to make the ride last longer. We were barely moving, but no cars were behind us. "Can we just forget what happened today, Nina?" she said.

That was just what I wanted too. I saw two girls younger than me, in about fifth or sixth grade, skating down the sidewalk. They were holding hands with each other and going as fast as they could. "But *why* won't you let me do things with my friends from school?" I asked. "What's so bad about it?" For once I was more curious than anything else. I really wanted to know what was on Joyce's mind.

"I just worry," she said. "I don't want anything to happen to you. In case you don't realize it, kiddo, you're all I've got."

"Nothing's going to happen to me."

"That's what you think," said Joyce. "You have no idea of the dangers of the world."

Both of us got out of the van and slammed doors. I didn't know what dangers she meant; all I could picture was Daryl Carpenter's face.

11 As things turned out, it was really convenient that Daryl and I lived so near each other. Starting in April, we began spending every afternoon together. His father was at work and his mother didn't live with them, so we'd go over to his house until six, which is when Joyce wanted me home. Daryl lived four streets away in a house that was even smaller than ours. He and his brother shared the only bedroom and his father slept on a roll-out couch.

In all the time we were seeing each other, I never met his father and Daryl never met Joyce. That was fine with me. As far as Joyce knew, I was with my girlfriends, at one of their houses. She said we could try this as long as I was home on time and she had a number where she could reach me. Every time the phone rang at Daryl's, I answered it, but she never did call.

I think Joyce had really scared herself that morning at McDonald's. We had a talk about it a few days later and Joyce told me she never wanted anything like that to happen again between us.

"Then let me do what I want after school," I said. "If you punish me, I'll only sneak around again." I didn't mean to threaten her, but it was the truth. By that point I was desperate to see Daryl and would have done almost anything.

Joyce was quiet for a long time. We were sitting on the front steps before supper, and I could hear the birds singing and somebody's radio playing from an open window. "All right," she finally said. "We'll give it a try."

I told Joyce I was at a girlfriend's just to make things easier, but if she'd known I was at Daryl's, I'm not even sure she would have minded. Joyce is a weird mixture, as I've said, and in some ways she's more open-minded than other parents. I remember something she said once about a minister on the radio who was preaching against teenagers. "He might as well tell birds not to fly. Kids that age are like magnetic poles. They're going to get together, no matter what."

At first Daryl and I mainly watched television. For some reason he loved the soap operas and had been keeping up with one of them, *Guiding Light*, since he was a little boy. They always had a big supply of sodas in that house, and Daryl would get us Cokes and we'd sit on the couch (the same one his father slept on), watching the show. Usually Joel was there too, and Daryl would put his arm around me and explain who the characters were and all the dirty deals they'd pulled on each other in the past. There was a lot of sex in these soap operas too, but we didn't discuss that.

Since Joyce and I had never had television, it was kind of a novelty, but I couldn't understand exactly what Daryl and I were doing together and I kept waiting for something else to happen. Aside from our comments about the television, we really didn't say much.

But one afternoon a few weeks after I started going over there, he suddenly led me into his bedroom and began kissing me like crazy. He kissed me on my face and my hair and my neck, long kisses that made me feel weak and helpless, as if I had no will of my own and would just fall to the floor in a heap. "Can we sit down?" I finally managed to whisper.

He took me over to the bed then and kept kissing me. I guess I kissed him back a few times, but mainly it was him kissing me. After about an hour of this, some change in the way the sun was coming through the window shades made me realize it was getting late. "Daryl, I think we should stop," I said.

He pulled back and looked at me. His eyes were blue. I should mention that because until I'd started going to his house I'd never seen him without his sunglasses. "Yeah, sure. Sorry," he said.

It turned out it wasn't even five-thirty, but I discovered I wanted to go home anyway. We went back into the living room and Daryl adjusted the volume on the television. "See you later," he said as I walked out the door.

On the way back to my house, I worried about what was going to happen tomorrow. Would anything be different between Daryl and me or would he just say, "Oh, hi," as if he'd never kissed me, never had his face pressed up to mine? I still had a vivid sensation of that because he must already shave and the hair of his cheeks had rubbed my skin and irritated it a little.

So when I first came inside and Joyce said, "Who have you been kissing?" I put my hand up to cover my face.

"No, not there," she said. "Go look in the mirror."

I went into the bathroom and turned on the light over the sink. On the right side of my neck were two bruises, round black-and-blue marks as big as quarters. The sight was so shocking that I immediately turned the light off, but their afterimage stayed with me, floating in the dark. Joyce had come into the bathroom too. "You told me you were at a friend's house," she said. "You didn't get those from a friend."

"But what are they?" I asked.

Joyce laughed and I realized then that I could say what I wanted and she wouldn't get upset.

"We used to call them hickeys. I have no idea what they're called now. Come on, kiddo," she said, "let's start supper."

I followed her into the kitchen. "But when will they go away? Will I still have them tomorrow?"

"I think it takes a few days. They turn brownish yellow and then they disappear."

I sat down at the table and ate some Triscuits and cheese. Meanwhile Joyce was shaping hamburger meat into patties. She'd taken out everything for a salad too, but she didn't ask me to help. I think she wanted my company more than anything else.

Hickeys . . . what an ugly word. I went over to

Joyce's mirror behind the front door to see if they were as bad as I thought. But they were worse, darker and more raw-looking and too high on my neck to even be covered by a turtleneck.

That night I couldn't eat much supper. "I don't feel well," I told Joyce. "Can I stay home from school tomorrow?"

"Forget it," she said. "You know how I feel about cutting school."

"Please. Just this once," I pleaded.

She took a beer out of the refrigerator and peered across the table at me. "If it's those hickeys you're worried about, you'd be amazed at what a good concealer and some powder can do. I'll show you how to put it on. Just stay out of the sunshine tomorrow and nobody will notice."

Well she was right. Nobody noticed, especially not Daryl. He was ahead of me as usual in the morning, waiting at our bus stop with Joel. The weather had warmed up and both of them were wearing blue jeans and white T-shirts that looked like they'd just been ironed. "How ya doin'?" said Daryl.

"Fine." I was aware of my trembly smile and I was trying not to feel too shy. We stood there for two or three minutes, but neither of us said another word. Joel and Daryl talked to each other a little, but that was it.

When the bus came, I was careful to sit on the right-hand side with my hickeys toward the window. I expected Daryl to sit with me. We'd been sitting together on the bus for the last three weeks. But on this day Daryl walked past me and sat next to his brother instead.

I could feel tears starting up in my eyes. I couldn't figure it out. I tried not to panic, but all I could think was that he had kissed me yesterday and now for some reason we weren't going together anymore. I looked out the window. The tears in my eyes made the scenery blurry, but I watched it anyway, trying hard not to cry.

When we got to school, Daryl was the first one off the bus. He rushed past me and disappeared inside the school building before I'd even left my seat. Kids streamed up the walkways in twos and threes, clowning around and laughing. No one said a word to me and I didn't talk to anyone either.

Ever since that day with Joyce at McDonald's, Daryl was the only person I spent time with at school. I stayed next to him every second I was in the lunchroom or the school yard and I waited for him outside the doors of my classes so we could walk in the halls together. His presence was so strong, I felt like it kept other people away from me.

The first week I was going with Daryl, Nancy and Doris and Laureen kept trying to talk to me, but I didn't respond to any of their remarks except to say yes or no. I even asked my teachers if I could change my seat in classes. Finally the three of them got the point.

If you really want to know though, the whole episode made me sad. Those girls, and Nancy especially, had been nicer to me than anyone my own age except for Sam Gordon, but Joyce had ruined that for me, and now the time I'd spent being their friend seemed part of another life.

No other girls had come forward to take their place, that was for sure. By going with Daryl, at first I thought I'd automatically get in with the other rockers, but it hadn't worked that way. All the girls had it in for me, I don't know why, maybe they were jealous. I tried to change my style to conform with theirs and I acted really friendly whenever I was around them, but nothing made a difference. I tried not to let it bother me though. I was with Daryl and they weren't.

As I went through my classes that morning, I kept hoping that Daryl and I would get back together at lunchtime. Usually we sat at a table by ourselves, except sometimes Joel came over with a friend from sixth grade. I should have known better though. Because when I walked into the cafeteria, Daryl was eating his lunch at the rockers' group table and all the other seats were taken.

Outside in the school yard it would be even worse. Rimmed by its chain-link fence, the whole place was like a giant stage where everyone was an actor and everyone saw everything. Who was I going to stand with now? Nancy and Laureen and Doris were on top of the iron stairway, that hadn't changed, but climbing up there would be impossible.

It was a hot day and the sun blinded me at first when I came outside through the basement door. But I thought I saw Daryl turn his back to me and walk away. If he was expecting me to go over to him or cause a scene, he didn't know me at all.

This wouldn't be the first time I'd been completely on my own in a school and I knew it wouldn't be the last either. But something about the pain I felt was different from when I was younger. It wasn't only that Daryl and I had broken up. Instead there seemed to be nowhere left for me to turn.

My classes that afternoon went by slowly. I could see the hands of the clocks move and hear the clicking sound they made as each minute passed. I was completely distracted, waiting for the day to be over. And then on my way to English last period, I bumped into Corinne Yancy on the stairs.

It was an accident, but not according to Corinne. She was a rocker, a tough seventh grader who bleached her hair and weighed about twice as much as me. "Watch where you're going!" she yelled and she slammed into me so hard with her shoulder that I tripped and almost lost my balance.

As my books and purse slid slowly down the stairs, she glanced over at me and said, "Maybe next time you'll be more careful." I wondered if she might mean something about Daryl. That's how paranoid I was at the time.

But it didn't matter. Suddenly I'd had enough. I walked the rest of the way down the stairs, past the principal's office, and out the door of the school. And then I started running. This move on my part was unplanned, I swear it. The sun was beating down on the asphalt streets and soon my heart was pounding and sweat was breaking out on my face and chest.

I ran on the empty sidewalks beside the quiet neighborhoods until I was nearly home. An old man was planting flowers and I saw a woman taking care of little kids and hanging up laundry. It all seemed far from my life but I waved to them as I passed.

I pictured telling Joyce what had happened, all about Daryl, everything. But she'd been acting so unpredictable lately that I didn't dare. So I bypassed our street and ran up onto the canyon road that led toward Bear Lake. I'd been curious about it since we'd moved here, and anyway I had until six to be home.

12 I was in gym class the next morning when I heard my name being broadcast over the PA system. "Nina Lewis, please come to the principal's office. Nina Lewis, you're wanted in the office at once."

"Should I change out of my gym clothes?" I asked my teacher. We were doing a gymnastics unit and I wasn't all that sweaty.

She looked me over. "No, you might as well go the way you are."

I didn't know what to expect. They took attendance in the mornings and I was pretty sure no one had seen me leave last period yesterday. Plus my grades were good. On my report card I hadn't gotten under a B in anything.

The halls were deserted as I walked through them. But when I turned a corner past the science lab, I suddenly came face to face with Daryl. Both of us were so startled that we just stood there for a moment and stared at each other. Then Daryl dropped his gaze. "Hey, listen. I'm sorry," he said. "It's nothing against you."

"I know." It was true. Really I *did* know. I hadn't liked what was happening between us either, the way I'd become so helpless and afraid to talk to him. He must have thought I was really boring. Even when he'd kissed me, I'd kept my arms at my sides like it meant nothing to me. I regretted that now, but of course it was too late.

Daryl held up his hall pass. This showed that the person had five minutes out of class to use the bathroom. "Well, see you around I guess." He ran up the stairs away from me, taking them two at a time.

I felt pretty shaken up. Well put it this way, it wasn't what I needed to happen, especially when I was on my way to the principal's office.

I'd only met this man once personally, on my first day of school at Logan, but kids said he was really strict and gave out detentions for the slightest thing. Believe it or not, his name was Mr. Kopp.

"Close the door behind you," the secretary said, pointing toward his office.

Mr. Kopp was waiting for me inside. So was Joyce. She was sitting facing him at his desk and I remembered our other time there and how she was wearing her suit. Today she had on a cherry red skirt and sweater to match. She gave me a big smile when she saw me and that made me feel reassured.

"Please sit down, Nina," said Mr. Kopp, sweeping his hand out to show me the only empty chair in the room. "It has come to my attention that you were not with us yesterday afternoon during last period." He waited but I did not answer.

"Where were you, Nina?"

"I went home early." I looked at Joyce but she didn't contradict me, even though it had been almost six when I got home last night. I'd probably run four miles on the canyon road plus however many miles it was on my way from school.

"Mr. Kopp has other concerns too," said Joyce.

"Frankly, Nina, we're worried about you." Mr. Kopp

stood up and began walking back and forth behind his desk. "Why did you tell Doris Baker your father was killed in a car accident?"

I felt my heart start racing. I couldn't believe he'd found out something like that.

"You know, there's nothing wrong with the fact that your father and I are divorced," Joyce said. "You don't have to lie about it to your friends."

Neither did she have to lie about it! But I certainly couldn't say that in Mr. Kopp's office. In the leather-covered armchair, Joyce crossed her legs and smoothed her skirt. Then I saw that Mr. Kopp was watching her and I realized she was doing it on purpose.

"Nina is a fine girl. Make no mistake about that, Mrs. Lewis. Her teachers say her work is excellent and she's certainly not a behavior problem. That's why I called you in today. Has she mentioned a boy named Daryl Carpenter?"

"Not that I can recall."

"It's a sad story really. His mother deserted the home when the two boys were still babies. I'm sure the father did the best he could with them, but under the circumstances . . ."

"I understand," said Joyce.

"I'll be frank with you, Mrs. Lewis. There's a group of children in this school that the other children call rockers. They act like little hoodlums. Problem kids, all of them. Daryl Carpenter is one of the leaders. If

I were you, I would not want my daughter associating with him."

Joyce stood up then as if he'd suddenly announced the meeting was over. "Thank you for calling me, Mr. Kopp." She slung her purse over her shoulder. "I'm sure Nina and I will have a lot to talk about when she comes home today."

Alone in the room, the principal and I faced each other across his desk. For the first time he really seemed to notice me. "I gather you were in gym class, young lady. You'd better hurry and get back there."

"What a ridiculous man!" said Joyce. We were riding our bikes to a Chinese restaurant. It had been her idea, both to eat out and to take the bikes.

"You mean Mr. Kopp?"

"The nerve of him! Telling me how to bring you up!"

It was a quiet evening with a warm wind. We were riding down the main shopping strip, where all the big stores and restaurants and shopping centers were. There was almost no traffic and I thought I knew the reason. This was probably the one night every week that Mormons were supposed to stay home. Family Home Evening, they called it. Only stray people or weird isolated little families like Joyce and me were likely to be around tonight.

Stray people was right! Because when we got to the

shopping center where the Chinese restaurant was (it was the only Chinese restaurant in town), who should I see but a big group of rockers from my school. They all had their bikes and they were just hanging out, smoking cigarettes and flirting and laughing. Luckily Daryl wasn't there, but Corinne Yancy was and so were a lot of other kids who knew me.

Last week it would have killed me to be seen riding my ten-speed with my mother. But now I didn't even care. Why should I? Daryl was already gone.

Joyce and I locked our bikes to a rack outside a Quik Foto store and walked across the parking lot to the restaurant. I thought Joyce hadn't noticed the kids, even though they were pretty hard to miss with their tight clothes and aggressive presence. But after we'd been seated in the restaurant for a while and were reading our menus, she suddenly said, "I bet those were rockers."

"Right." I hoped this would be the end of the conversation, but no such luck.

"Do you like that style?"

"What style?"

"You know, like punks or outlaws or something."

"It's better than looking like everyone else," I said. "Most of the kids around here act like they're about ten years old. They're babies," I said.

"I have an idea, Nina." Joyce leaned forward and cupped her hands around the candle on our table. I noticed it was shaped like a little pagoda. "Do you think you can last here until the end of school?" she said.

"What?" I said. I was stalling for time. I could not believe that basically she'd announced we were going to be moving again. I couldn't take it in.

In spite of how terrible my life in Logan had become, the last thing in the world I wanted was to go somewhere else. Lately it was clear to me that moving only made things worse, it only put you more on the outside and made you stranger and more lonely than you were before. If I knew that already, why didn't Joyce know it too?

"There's this place in California you'll love, Nina. It's got everything. It's right next to the Pacific Ocean. And the people are so sophisticated, there are thousands of them, almost a city of people, and no two are alike. In that place your *rockers* will look like babies. I swear it, you'll be amazed."

I felt like I was going to either break something or start crying. I pictured smashing my arm into the table and shattering the plates and teacups, scattering the silverware through the air.

"How are you this evening?" The waitress had come to take our order. She was standing beside me with her pad and pencil in her hands.

"What do you want to eat?" asked Joyce.

"Do they have lo mein?"

"Shrimp, pork, chicken, and beef," said the waitress. "What kind do you want?"

"I'll have pork," I answered.

"Make that two," said Joyce. "And some egg drop soup for both of us."

I used to love egg drop soup when I was little. There was one restaurant when we lived in Toronto where Joyce used to get it to go, in white paper containers, on her way home from work. We had a next-door neighbor then who used to take care of me after school, and Janice, her daughter, was really nice. At that time I felt like I had everything I wanted, a friend my own age to play with and my mother every night.

Toronto was fine too, there was nothing the matter with the city. We could have just stayed there. "Oh, I've lived here since I was five," I'd be able to say now if anyone ever asked me. And I'd pronounce "about" as "aboat," the way they did in Canada.

I thought of other places I'd loved. There was one town, Dubuque, Iowa, that I always remember for its big, slow-moving river and a wonderful teacher I had in third grade named Mrs. Green. And Montpelier too, of course. If I could have played basketball there and gone out with Sam Gordon, I felt like I would have been happy forever.

Joyce reached out across the table and took my hand. "You've been so quiet, Nina. What are you thinking?"

It was probably hopeless, but still I said, "I don't want to do it anymore. I don't want to move again."

"You're right. I know what you mean, Nina. I understand perfectly. You've gotten too old for me to cart around the country anymore. I can see that. But still, you can't really expect us to stay in *Logan*."

The waitress brought our soup and Joyce stopped talking until she'd gone back into the kitchen. We were almost the only people in the restaurant, but she kept her voice to a whisper. "This will be the last time we move until you're finished with high school, I promise. Have I ever promised you that before?"

"Where's this place in California you were talking about?" I asked.

"Venice. It's near Los Angeles. You'll see, in Venice we'll be close again. We'll have so much fun together!" Joyce hadn't touched her soup and her face looked flushed and vivid.

"Can we at least wait till school is over?" I asked.

"Absolutely," said Joyce. "I already said that."

"How do you know about Venice?"

"I used to live there for a while," said Joyce. "It was a long time ago, I was still in my twenties."

Now this really surprised me. We'd never lived anywhere Joyce had lived before. At least not as far as I knew. But then Joyce was full of mysteries. She always had been.

One thing in Logan I was really going to miss was my tower room. I felt like I had to begin preparing myself to leave it behind. That night when Joyce and I got

home from the restaurant, I picked up my clothes and
cleaned it up completely. Then I opened all eight
windows and turned out the lights. When my eyes got
used to the darkness I could just make out the mountains, a jagged outline against the sky. I put my arms
around Silky and concentrated on the sensation of
being surrounded by air. There were some new night
sounds, maybe peepers had started up. I regretted that
I'd never see summer in this room.

After I'd been there for about an hour, Joyce
knocked on my door. "Can I turn on the light?" she
asked when she came in.

"Okay," I said. I had to close my eyes and open
them gradually, I'd been so long in darkness. But when
my vision cleared, I saw she was holding a letter.

"This came for you two weeks ago," said Joyce.

It had to be from Sam Gordon. Great! I'd been
wondering when he was going to write, especially
lately. I reached out to take the letter.

"Not so fast," said Joyce. "You're lucky I'm giving
you this at all. I didn't have to, you know. I could
have thrown it away."

"What do you mean? It's my letter."

"Did I ever say you could write people and let them
know where we were? I don't remember telling you
that."

The slow, quiet way she was talking made me very
uneasy. There were times with Joyce when you didn't

want to cross her, and this was definitely one of them. "I'm sorry," I said.

"Maybe you didn't mean to do anything wrong, but if you want me to give you more freedom and to be treated like an adult, there are certain things you're going to have to understand." She sat down next to me on the bed then. "I promised you before that once we move to Venice, we're going to stay there, right?"

I nodded. She was still holding the letter from Sam and I wondered if she was going to give it to me or not.

"Well, I need your help in return. No more letters to old boyfriends, no phone calls to old boyfriends. I don't know who this Sam Gordon is who wrote you or anything about Daryl Carpenter either. But it doesn't matter. There will be plenty of boys, dozens of them before you grow up.

"As far as school goes, I want you to stay out of trouble. Just go to your classes and get good grades, the way you always have. Don't give anyone a reason to wonder too much about you or to call me in. I don't want to sit in another principal's office."

I could understand that, but if Venice was really a city, the way she said, I doubted if anyone would be very interested in me.

"It's getting late now," said Joyce. "Here's your letter. After you read it, you better go right to bed."

When I opened the envelope the first thing I saw

was Sam's picture. It was a class picture, one of those little ones taken against a background painted to look like the sky. His hair had just been combed and it looked like he was trying not to smile. That made *me* smile.

> *Dear Nina,*
> *I was really glad to hear from you after so long. I'm glad you like Utah. My parents and brother and I are driving cross-country this summer and my parents said we can visit you. We wouldn't stay with you or anything, we have a camper. Probably we'd be getting there in the middle of July. My mother says to let us know if it's all right with your mother.*
> *Forget the girls' basketball team! They lost at least half the games they played. Our record was 9–12, which isn't bad for being the smallest school in the division. Mr. Jenks was really glad to know things were working out for you. He told me to tell you to keep growing and keep playing basketball. Actually I'm growing too. Maybe when I see you this summer we'll be the same height.*
> *I feel embarrassed about sending you this picture, but it's the only one my mother would let me have. How was your friend's birthday party? It sounded great.*
> *Write back soon. Don't wait a month this time.*
> *Love,*
> *Sam*

It was very exciting to me to think that he'd actually come here this summer to see me with his whole family. But by that time we'd be long gone. I guess the best thing to do was what Joyce said . . . just look ahead and find new boyfriends. I actually didn't know what other choice I had.

I took one more look at Sam's picture and I read his letter one more time. Then I put them in a special little chest where I kept all my sunset pictures and some glass animals I used to collect.

When I was done, I put the key to the chest back in my jewelry box, under the velvet bottom. I liked to think no one could open the chest except me. It was probably an illusion, but I liked to think so anyway. There were still some things I treasured.

✎ Part Three

Venice, California

13 Once when I was seven years old, Joyce took me to the circus in Cincinnati. I still remember it perfectly—the jugglers with their shiny balls, dancers in spangled tutus balancing on horses, clowns tripping and tumbling over one another. In every ring something different and all of it so exciting you didn't know where to look.

Well that was what Venice, California, was like. I could see without a doubt why Joyce had been drawn back here. It was a terrible mistake she made, but still I can understand it.

Our trip out from Utah was long and dry. Nevada and Southern California are a really hot part of the country anyway, and the end of June isn't the best time to travel. The van isn't air-conditioned. It wound up that we drove at night and slept in shaded rest areas during the day with the windows open and sheets put over them to shield us even more.

As it happened, we arrived in Venice on a Saturday. The freeways kept getting more and more crowded as we saw signs for Los Angeles and then finally there was a sign that said Venice/Santa Monica. At the first traffic light we stopped at, Joyce put on lipstick and combed her hair, and that's how I knew we were almost there. A gospel song was blasting from a loudspeaker outside a video store. They didn't have music like this in Utah.

"I think we should park the van in a lot for the next few days. Just until we get settled," said Joyce. "Then at night we can take it out and sleep down by the boardwalk."

The boardwalk. That was the first place in Venice she took me to. We got snow cones from a concession stand and strolled along with Silky on her leash, just gawking like all the other tourists.

On one side of us was a wide beach and the ocean, and on the other side was a row of outdoor stands with awnings. A stand might sell only mobiles made of shells or sunglasses or T-shirts. Actually T-shirts seemed to be the most popular item on the boardwalk. I saw one that I really liked. It said "Life's a Beach," and when I asked Joyce if I could have it, all she wanted to know was what color I wanted, she didn't even ask the price. (It was $8.99.)

Like in a circus, people were wearing costumes and seemed to be performing different acts for an audience. I guess we were part of the audience so I didn't feel too rude about staring. Two men with long hair and hoop earrings were riding a bicycle built for two; a woman in a polka-dot bikini was roller-skating with headphones on. I saw a woman in a blonde wig carrying a French poodle. Silky jumped up to see it, and we had to apologize. We saw real performers too—jugglers and musicians who were performing for money, and an artist who was doing a drawing with colored chalk on the sidewalk. That was also for money. She had a straw hat next to her with some quarters and dollar bills in it.

Up and down the boardwalk there were a lot of true punkers with their hair dyed orange and purple. There were crowds of Black people too, and some others with lighter skin and straight hair who Joyce said were Mexicans.

The place was amazing in every way. After about an hour of walking and looking, maybe you can understand why I finally said to Joyce, "Yes, but I don't get it. Does anyone really live here?"

For some reason my remark amused her. "Do you know how funny you are, kiddo?" She gave me a hug right in the middle of everyone. "I think it's time we went swimming," she said.

She was carrying a straw bag and now she took out my bathing suit and handed it to me. We got changed in a public pavilion on the beach and then ran down to the water. Actually I'd never been swimming in the ocean before. We'd stopped at the Great Salt Lake on our way out here, but it wasn't the same at all. This was the Pacific Ocean and you could look out to the horizon and see nothing but the red ball of the sun and a few white waves and sea gulls.

As it got later, people began leaving the beach and the air grew still and misty. I lay down on our beach towel and I must have slept for a while, because when I woke up, there was a picnic supper next to me with hero sandwiches and cans of lemonade and ice tea. Joyce was swimming parallel to the shore, I could see her red bathing cap flashing in and out of the water. It was the first time she'd left my side all day.

After we had eaten and changed back to our regular clothes, she showed me the rest of Venice, the part where people really lived. The houses were close together like in a city, but each had its own yard with flowers growing and weird tropical trees and bushes. There were real canals, too, like in Venice, Italy. Back here it seemed pretty and quiet, and in spite of some of the strange people we saw walking around, it had a settled feeling, like a real neighborhood.

"Do you think you might still know anyone here?" I asked Joyce.

"No," she answered, and she turned to go into a

drugstore. They usually don't allow dogs so I waited by the door with Silky.

"But how do you know you don't?" I said when she came back out. She was carrying a small paper bag. I looked inside and it had new toothbrushes for us both.

"What are you talking about, Nina?"

"How can you be sure you don't know anyone in Venice? You used to live here, right?"

"Yes," said Joyce, "but that was over twenty years ago. And anyway I only lived here for six or seven months."

I realized we were walking toward the parking lot where our van was. It was beginning to get really dark now and Joyce was walking along like we were in a race.

"Will you show me the place you used to live?" I asked her. I don't know why I was so excited about this, except I wanted to fill in part of the past, just one actual physical piece of it. Joyce had a little photograph album, like a diary, where she kept pictures of her parents and her brother and some pictures of me when I was little. I was always much more interested in the pictures of my grandparents. These two thin smiling people held a key to Joyce and me too. I used to think that if I only looked at them long enough, I could discover it. And now that we were in Venice, I felt the same way about seeing where Joyce had lived.

"It's summer. There's plenty of time for everything,"

she said as we got in our van and drove off. The parking lot had big lights on it and the door to the parking attendant's booth was locked. It crossed my mind that it might be dangerous here.

A full moon had risen when we got back down to the ocean. Along the beach, people were sleeping with big bags and bundles beside them. There were single people and couples and families with children too. "Why are they sleeping on the beach?" I asked Joyce.

"They're vagrants. They don't have anywhere else to go."

Suddenly for once I felt lucky. Inside the van our mattresses were made up with clean sheets and blankets. There was even a blanket for Silky. We closed the curtain that hung behind the front seat and got undressed by the light of the flashlight we always used. Joyce rolled down the two front windows just a little and I thought I could hear waves breaking on the shore.

"What were you doing in Venice the last time?" I whispered to Joyce as we lay in bed side by side. I knew she didn't like me asking her a lot of questions, but I couldn't seem to let it go. "What made you come here?"

She was quiet for so long that I thought she wasn't going to answer. But finally she said, "I came out here with a man. He wanted to get work at the studios."

"The studios?"

"You know, the movies," she said. "He was a lighting technician."

"But what did you do?"

"Me? I got a job as a waitress and supported us both."

"What happened to him?" I asked.

"I have no idea," Joyce said. "I got fed up and left. Now go to sleep, Nina. It's past eleven."

I wondered if she was telling me the truth. But it sounded too realistic to be a lie.

For the next four days we looked for a place to live. But we didn't see anything for under $500 a month and it began to look pretty hopeless. Joyce was even saying we should try some other places named Manhattan Beach and Redondo Beach, but I refused. "I'd rather just keep sleeping in the van," I said.

I'd been watching the life that kids my age had in Venice and all I wanted was for us to settle down so that I could have it too. Bands of kids rolled by us every day on bikes and skateboards and roller skates. I saw them down on the beach near the lifeguard stations early in the morning, everyone with great tans and the boys carrying their surfboards to the water.

Mornings were the best in Venice. That was before the tourists arrived. Joyce and I would eat breakfast in a doughnut shop on Pacific Avenue and then we'd buy the paper and start looking for places to rent. One morning we saw a two-room apartment we could afford, but the landlady told us she thought she'd rent it to a young couple who were on the way over. Joyce didn't have a job. I think that was the problem. But in new towns we usually tried to find a place before she looked for work—at least then she'd have an address to give the employer.

It was strange though. Since we'd been in Venice, she'd mentioned several times that she might not even get a job this summer. I myself didn't see how we'd manage if she didn't work, but then Joyce never would say exactly how much money she had. Probably no parents do.

We were headed back toward the beach on one of the streets behind the boardwalk. They were so narrow, cars couldn't even go there. We passed a house with an open front porch and I saw a woman about Joyce's age sitting outside with a cup of coffee. The day was so sunny and nice that I smiled at her and said "Hi," without even thinking about it.

The woman smiled back. She had a small pretty face and dark hair cut as short as a boy's. "Beautiful morning, isn't it?" she said.

Then Joyce did something that really surprised me. She walked over to the gate and undid the latch. "Could we come in?" she said, but she was already inside. She introduced herself to the woman and told her we were looking for a place to live. "For under four hundred dollars," she said. "You don't know of anything, do you?"

The woman stepped off her porch, still carrying her cup of coffee. "Where did you live before?" she asked.

"Logan, Utah. It's in the north. I was working for a newspaper, but I got laid off. I decided Nina would like Venice so we moved here. This is Nina," she said.

"Nice to meet you. My name's Margot Rose." The woman squinted against the bright sunlight as she looked us over and then she seemed to make up her mind about something. "Why don't you come up onto the porch," she said. "It's cooler."

We all sat in some wicker chairs and Margot and Joyce began to talk to each other about their lives. I was amazed at the things they said without knowing each other. Margot told Joyce she was a dancer but now she was too old for it and mainly taught dancing to children. She said she'd been lonely for three years, ever since she'd gotten divorced. Joyce told Margot about her job and the Mormons in Logan. I noticed she made it seem as though we'd lived there a long time, although she never actually said that.

Two cute boys went by, walking their bicycles. My mind started wandering. The day before we'd left Logan, I'd gone over to Daryl Carpenter's to say good-bye. I wanted him to know I was leaving. I wondered if he had anything more to say to me—there might be a lesson for me in what had happened. When I got to his house though, a whole bunch of kids were in the living room. I could see them through the screen door.

Daryl had his arm around a girl named Edie Sparks. I walked away, I didn't even knock.

Joyce and Margot got up, pushing back their chairs. "Aren't you coming?" asked Joyce. "Margot just asked if we wanted to see her house."

"Sure," I said.

"She's got a room for rent. Her son's away at college."

"I know." I'd heard them talking about it, but I wasn't really listening. The idea of sharing a room with Joyce and of living in someone else's house seemed so unlikely.

"Sometimes he comes home on weekends, but the attic's finished and he can stay there," said Margot. "I already told him I might rent his room. I told him we needed the money." Margot led us down a white hallway. On the walls were some framed photographs of her in dancer's tights and leotards. Her hair was long in the pictures and she wore it pulled back from her face. I thought she looked much better now but I didn't say anything.

Her son's room was in the back of the house, looking over a courtyard. It had two beds and a straw rug on the floor. Almost nothing else was in it. "Well, what do you think?" asked Margot.

"Nina?" said Joyce.

I was mad she'd put me in this position. At least she could have said we'd talk about it and let Margot know later. I shrugged and didn't answer.

"Well, *I* think it's a great idea. As long as we can rent it week by week with no lease."

"That's fine with me." said Margot.

They began to discuss the details. Margot wanted only $50 a week, which would really save us money, and we could use her kitchen to cook in. I saw the advantages of this setup and I told myself I should be happy about it. Joyce had gone out of her way to make a friend, and to me that was another sign that she meant what she said and we were really going to stay in Venice.

Still, something about the way things were going bothered me. If Joyce didn't work, it would be hard enough having my own life every day, but at Margot's we'd even be sleeping in the same room at night. I felt like Joyce was pulling me closer and closer. She was giving me Venice but she'd trapped me here too.

14

It was the beach that saved me. It was only a block from Margot's house and no one minded if I went there as long as it was light out. I got into the habit of going to bed early, at about nine. Joyce and Margot would still be in the living room, talking and drinking wine. Or as time went on, they began going

out at night together. I'm not sure where they went
exactly, probably to bars.

Anyway I'd set my alarm for five and keep it under
the covers with me so that it wouldn't wake Joyce.
Then I'd get up, take some fruit from a bowl Margot
kept in the kitchen, and hit the beach running. If you
like running, there's nowhere better than the beach.
I ran barefoot, always in the same direction, toward
the Santa Monica hills. By the time I came back, the
waves would be cresting and the surfers would be out.

I really wanted to make friends with these confident
California kids. But even though I stood near them
and watched them morning after morning, they never
said a word to me. Margot told me that the bands of
surfers were very rigid about who they let in, almost
like street gangs in New York City. The girls with
them had grown up with them. So I tried not to take
it personally.

I was pretty lonely though. My last month of school
in Logan I'd barely talked to anyone, and now with
Joyce always around, it seemed like I might not meet
any kids my age in Venice either. But one morning
about a week after we moved in with Margot, I was
running on the beach when I suddenly heard someone
running behind me. The sand muffled the sound, but
I could hear the person's breathing. I slowed down but
he didn't pass me. When I speeded up, he speeded up
too. For a mile or more he stayed right behind me,
just beyond my field of vision. I can't tell you how I

knew it was a boy. I just did, that's all. Finally I got too curious about who he was so I stopped running. He skidded past me and turned around, laughing.

I was very surprised by his appearance. All he had on were running shoes and cutoffs. Whoever made the cutoffs had just hacked them off unevenly and the strings hung halfway to his knees. His hair was long, at least as long as mine, and he was wearing a rolled-up bandanna around his forehead like an Indian brave in a movie. But what was most startling was his height. He must have been six and a half feet tall.

"What's so funny?" I asked. We were walking side by side now, but he was still laughing.

"It's hard to say. Some things just strike me funny, that's all."

"Like me, you mean?" I was getting annoyed. I'd been looking for someone to spend time with, but he wasn't who I had in mind.

"Nah, it's not you. I just have a weird sense of humor."

"I guess so."

"Listen, don't be mad. Do you want to go out for breakfast? I know a good place," said the boy.

I looked at my watch. It was still before six. Joyce and Margot wouldn't be getting up for a while. "I don't have any money," I told him.

"That's all right. I'll pay."

We walked up the beach to a big open parking lot. Even though it was still early, vendors were there already, setting up tables and pulling furniture and boxes of dishes out of station wagons and trucks. This was Venice's flea market area. I'd wandered through it once or twice in my travels.

The boy—he'd told me his name was Artie—went up to an older couple who were just sitting on folding chairs on a strip of grass near the pavement. "These are my parents," he said. "Moe and Mary, this is Nina. We're going out to breakfast. Can I have five bucks?"

His father handed it over. "Bye-bye," I said, but neither one of them said good-bye.

"They're tired," said Artie. "We drove five hours to get here." He took me to a restaurant that must have been run by Arabs. It was a little stand, a shack really, with two tables outside under an awning. We both had strong sweet coffee and some kind of pastry made with honey and raisins. He ordered for me. It was the first time in my life I'd ever drunk coffee.

The hour was so early and the whole incident was so mysterious and dreamlike that I didn't even think to ask any questions. I just went along with whatever happened. After we ate, we went to see a friend of Artie's, a man who ran a jewelry shop on the board-walk. He was a small man who had a bushy beard, only he was completely bald. He was very nice to me and opened his shop to show me a pair of earrings I'd admired in the window. Silver stars dangled from crescent moons, and when I held them to my ears, I knew I really wanted them.

"My card," said the man, handing me a square of white paper.

"Lionel Winter, Silversmith," I read. "I'll show this to my mother. How late are you open?"

"Until nine during the week. Midnight on weekends."

Artie walked me back to our gate, but I wouldn't let him come to the house. He was too strange-looking, for one thing. I wondered how old he was. It was hard to tell because of his height. Artie said his parents lived in Fresno and only came to Venice on weekends for the flea market. He'd be there the next morning and we arranged to meet at the lifeguard station, but after that I wouldn't see him again for a week. That was all right with me. I needed some time to think about him.

I let myself in the front door with my key and tiptoed through the living room. But all my precautions were wasted because Joyce was already up. She was reading the newspaper and eating a peach. "Have a good run?" she asked. "You were gone a long time."

"I met a boy who took me out for breakfast." I wanted to see what she'd say, to get a feeling of what my limits here really were.

"What's his name?"

"Artie."

"Artie who?"

"I don't know," I admitted.

"Well, you should ask," said Joyce. And that was the end of it, I think because Margot came into the room. She was still in her nightgown and bathrobe even though we were both dressed. Margot took a relaxed attitude toward everything. I was really getting to like her.

Today she was supposed to teach some modern dance classes in Westwood, so Joyce and I were going to drive her. Her own car was being fixed. We planned to go shopping while we waited for her. Margot said that Westwood had great stores because it was right next to UCLA and all the college kids went shopping there.

But as it turned out, so did kids my age. After we dropped Margot, we parked the van inside a giant underground parking garage and took the escalator up four levels to the street. Actually we were in a plaza surrounded by shops. Kids were roaming everywhere. Most of them were wearing surfer clothes, even though I knew they couldn't all be surfers. In California that was just the style.

For about two hours Joyce and I went in and out of shops. They were all so glossy, they looked like stage sets from a movie. It was actually intimidating to think you could even buy anything, although I did succeed in getting two pairs of bright flowered shorts and an OP (for Ocean Pacific) sweatshirt. Joyce didn't buy

anything. She said she was looking for cotton sun-
dresses, but when it came time to go off on her own
and try some on, she never did it. She seemed more
interested in what I was going to buy.

"Are you sure we can afford this?" I asked her. The
OP sweatshirt was forty dollars and I'd just seen a pair
of Nike running shoes I wanted too.

"Let me worry about that."

"But you're not even working," I said. Joyce really
does tend to be extravagant and I didn't want us to
run out of money. That was what happened in Dubuque. We got so poor there that finally the only
solution was to move.

"Did you hear me, Nina?"

"Yes." We were standing in a big sporting goods
store within earshot of everyone. Two girls who were
looking at tennis rackets glanced at us curiously.

"What did I say?" said Joyce.

"You said to let you worry about it."

"Right. Now which running shoes were they?"

I put the Nikes I wanted out of my mind and showed
Joyce a much cheaper pair. She didn't run, she'd never
know the difference.

We weren't supposed to pick Margot up until one
o'clock, but by twelve we were worn out. Finally we
just found a table on the plaza and sat with our shopping bags, waiting for the time to pass. It was quite a
spectacle anyway. You could see some pick-ups going
on and connections being made. I fantasized coming

here again after school started in the fall, when I'd
have a group of friends of my own.

I was going through my wallet, trying to see if I had
any change left to buy a fruit ice, when I came across
the card the jeweler had given me. I'd put it in my
wallet after I got home so that I wouldn't forget about
it. "Lionel Winter, Silversmith," I read.

"What did you say?" asked Joyce sharply.

"Lionel Winter, Silversmith. He's a jeweler I met
with the boy I told you about this morning."

"Let me see that," said Joyce, taking it out of my
hand. She looked at it and turned it over and felt the
edges with her thumb. "Why did he give you his card?"

"I saw some earrings I liked. They were beautiful,
Joyce, little stars hanging from crescent moons. They
were for pierced ears too."

"Did you want to buy them, you mean?"

"Well, I thought you might like to see them. He
had other really pretty things too."

Joyce collected our shopping bags and stood up. "I
don't think so," she said. "Let's go get Margot."

Her voice had an abrupt angry tone that didn't go
with the situation, and though I didn't think much
about it at the time, the next morning when I saw
Artie, I asked him if we could go back to Lionel's
store.

"Sure, if you want to," Artie said. "But I know
plenty of other interesting people besides him."

We were walking along the beach at the tide line.

I was picking up flat black stones and putting them in my pocket. Artie was picking them up too. Only he'd throw them back into the ocean, skipping the stones through the waves. Yesterday when Joyce and I were in Westwood, the image of tall Artie in his raggedy cutoffs had seemed odd and embarrassing to me. I almost decided not to show up at the lifeguard station at six like we'd arranged. But I knew that was wrong, and then when I actually saw him, I discovered I was glad.

We ate breakfast at the same restaurant as the day before and then we went to Lionel's. His apartment was on top of his store, but most of it was a workshop taken up with lengths of silver wire and cutting tools. "Ah, you've come back for the earrings," he said when he let us in.

"I wish. Actually . . . this is going to sound strange." I'd acted so impulsively, I hadn't really thought about what I was going to say beforehand. I made myself go on. "My mother used to live in Venice and I wondered if you knew her."

"Why?" asked Lionel. "Did she say she knew me?"

"No, but she acted strange when I showed her your card and I just thought . . ."

"What's your mother's name?" Lionel asked.

"Joyce Lewis. She's about five three and has red hair like mine. Well, actually she dyes it, it's really dark brown."

"No, I don't think I know her. When did she live in Venice?"

"Twenty or twenty-five years ago, I think." I was getting really self-conscious. I wished I hadn't come here.

"That's a long time ago," said Lionel gently. He walked over to the window and opened it. The curtains blew into the room and suddenly I could smell the sea.

Nobody spoke for a while and then Artie said, "Maybe we should get going. Probably Lionel's got work to do." As we were walking downstairs I felt a little dizzy as though I'd climbed too high up on a ladder or something. I wasn't sure if I should be glad or sorry not to have discovered a secret about Joyce. Why was I checking up on her anyway? At that point, I don't think I could even have explained it.

15

Every day in July Joyce and I went to the beach. Along the sand, built right into the sand actually, was a concrete bike path that went for miles. We'd take our bikes and pack a picnic in Joyce's straw bag and by nine in the morning we'd be on our way.

Those days were hot with the winds they called Santa Anas blowing from the desert, but in the mornings near the water it was always cool. We'd spread our beach towels and just lie in the sand like corpses, thinking our separate thoughts. I listened to my Walk-man a lot.

One day close to noontime I was almost asleep when something suddenly blocked the light. The color be-hind my eyes changed from orange to black and I thought the sun had gone behind a cloud. But then I heard a woman's voice. "You look just like someone I know."

At first I thought she meant me, but then I realized she was talking to Joyce. Something told me to keep my eyes shut.

"Oh, really? I don't think we've met." That was Joyce. She sounded like she wished the woman would go away.

"Isn't your name Georgia Halloran?"

"No, it's Joyce Lewis."

"But didn't you used to live in Venice in the sixties?"

"What is this?" said Joyce. "I don't see what business it is of yours."

"You look just like Georgia Halloran. Your voice is even the same," the woman persisted.

"Look, I said I don't know you. Now would you mind!" I could tell by Joyce's voice that she was really upset. She shook me roughly by the shoulder. "Come on, Nina, it's time to go."

When I opened my eyes, she was wildly throwing things into her bag, even the beach towels that were covered with sand. I looked around for the woman but she was already gone, vanished on the crowded beach.

One thing was for sure though. Joyce was in a big hurry to get out of there. She raced past me on her bicycle and I had to stand up and pedal like crazy to even keep her in sight. It was probably the fastest she'd moved in years.

I felt a little worried but mainly I was just curious. The first thing I wanted to know was who was Georgia Halloran. If Joyce didn't at least know her, why had she gotten so upset? Actually there was another time in Venice someone had called out to Joyce, thinking she was someone else. We were in our van on Electric Avenue (great name, right?) waiting for the light to change. A woman who was in the crosswalk ran up to us. "I can't believe it!" she said. "What are you doing here? Did you know they were looking for you?" I think she called Joyce some other name, too, but I've forgotten it. As a matter of fact, I'd forgotten the whole incident until that morning.

I wished I could just come right out and ask Joyce what was going on. But that would have been like trying to climb the Eiffel Tower barefoot. I knew I wasn't going to get anywhere.

That summer was a total loss as far as people my own age were concerned. Of course I still met Artie on Saturday and Sunday mornings, but he didn't really count since he lived so far away and I'd never see him again once we both went back to school.

I didn't like Artie as a boyfriend—at least that's

what I told myself. But his manner and weird looks
had begun to grow on me. Every time I saw him we
did something unique. Once he took me up into the
streets of Santa Monica. It was a rich suburb where
every lawn was bright green and every house looked
perfect. Of course at seven in the morning when we
were there, nobody was around except the rich people's
gardeners watering the lawns. *"Buenas días,"* said
Artie, greeting them in Spanish.

Another time we went to a marina, a kind of inlet
where people keep their boats. Artie knew a kid there
who was in charge of washing down the decks of the
big wooden cabin cruisers every morning. He gave us
a tour of one of them, and he and Artie talked about
pulling up anchor and taking it for a ride in the ocean.
"Count me out," I said, walking up the gangplank.

"We were just kidding," said the kid, whose name
was Allen.

"I don't think it's funny," I said. "We could get in
a lot of trouble." For some reason their attitude really
upset me and instead of waiting for Artie to come after
me, I ran home by myself. He yelled at me once to
come back, but I just kept going.

It was a Sunday and I figured I'd just meet him the
next weekend and explain, but instead at ten o'clock
that night there was a knock on our door. Joyce and
Margot and I were watching a movie on television,
and Margot got up to answer it.

The next thing I knew Artie was standing in our

living room. You could tell he'd made an effort to look
nice. His long hair was under a baseball cap and he
had on a plaid cotton shirt with a collar. Both these
items had probably come from the flea market. "Hi,
Nina," he said, flashing me a grin.

"And who might you be?" asked Joyce. She didn't
sound very friendly.

"Come on, Joyce," said Margot. "Aren't you even
going to ask him to sit down?"

"That's okay. Glad to meet you. I'm Artie." He
walked over to Joyce and shook her hand. Then he
shook Margot's. "Could Nina come out for a walk?"
he asked.

"It's ten o'clock at night," said Joyce. All this time
the television was still on. The hero and heroine in
the old movie we'd been watching were about to em-
brace. They were looking at each other longingly.

"Please, Joyce. Just for half an hour."

"She'll be back by ten-thirty, I promise," said Artie.

"As long as they don't go down to the beach,"
Margot told Joyce.

"We never would," I said.

Joyce stood up and turned off the television. "All
right." She sighed like she was doing us a big favor.
"Half an hour and no more."

Artie and I were halfway down the block (we were
walking to the boardwalk as usual) when he said,
"Which one was your mother?"

"Are you kidding? You mean you couldn't tell?" I was astounded! I felt like Joyce's hold over me was so strong, it attached us to each other like an actual rope or chain.

Artie just shrugged. "Was it the one who turned off the television?"

"Who else?"

"Well, it could have been the one who answered the door."

"You jerk," I said. "Are you serious?"

"No, I'm Artie."

See what I mean about him? How could you not get attached to a person like that? It turned out he'd asked his parents to stay over an extra night in Venice just so he could talk to me.

As we walked along the boardwalk with the surging weekend crowds, he said, "I bet you do that a lot."

"Do what?"

"You know, leave every time you don't know what else to do. Like at the marina this morning."

It was my impulse right then, I swear, to turn around and walk away from him. Especially after what he'd just said, it was so strong, it really shocked me.

I thought about all the times I'd taken off just in the past few years. On a rainy day in Seattle after a bad day at school, once in Fairbanks after someone hurt my feelings, in Montpelier that time Joyce had lied to me, in Logan in the canyon, running until I almost dropped. But now in California, smack up against the Pacific Ocean, it suddenly felt like there was no place left to go.

I started crying and Artie put his arms around me, but that only made it worse. I cried until my throat hurt and I was shuddering for breath. He led me over to some bleachers next to an empty basketball court and sat with me until I calmed down. The front of his shirt was soaking wet from my tears.

"Better now?" he said, taking my hand. "Look, I brought you something." Under the streetlights I suddenly saw Lionel Winter's crescent moon earrings shining in my palm.

"Oh, Artie." I had no words for this. I felt like I'd start crying again.

"Aren't you going to try them on?" He led me back to the boardwalk, to one of the stalls where they were selling sunglasses. A mirror had been set up for the customers. I took off my other earrings and put on the crescent moons. They looked beautiful to me, and when I turned to show Artie, I think he thought so too.

"But you shouldn't have spent so much money." That part was bothering me.

"Lionel gave them to me for much less. In a way they're a present from both of us. He really liked you."

We were walking back to Margot's house now. Our half hour was almost up. "Maybe next weekend when I see you, we can go thank him," I said.

"Sure, we can go on Saturday."

"You better not come in," I told Artie when we got to the garden gate.

"Hey, no problem." Artie put his hands up in the air and backed off as if someone were holding a gun on him. I'd been wondering if he was going to kiss me or what was going to happen. But all he did was keep backing down the street. "Next Saturday at the lifeguard station? The regular time?"

"Right," I said. When he was out of sight, I took off the crescent earrings and put them in my pocket. I didn't want Joyce to see them.

She and Margot were both sitting in the living room. They'd turned off the television and I noticed that they'd changed their clothes too. Both of them had on skirts and high heels and Joyce was wearing her rhinestone earrings.

"Where are you two going?"

"Just out for a while," said Joyce. She walked over to a mirror Margot had in the hallway and started fixing her hair. "That was good. You came back on time."

"He was cute, Nina," said Margot. "Nice smile. How old is he though?"

"I'm not sure."

"Joyce and I were thinking he must be at least seventeen."

"Oh, no! That's much too old! Why would he like me then?"

"Good question," said Margot.

"Has he tried anything?" said Joyce. But she was smiling as she said it.

"Joyce! Cut it out, you're embarrassing me! He's just tall for his age. Lots of kids are. He's probably only around fifteen."

"Why don't you ask him next time?" said Margot. "Not that it really matters." She turned off the overhead light in the kitchen. "Come on, Joyce, the place closes at midnight."

"Will you be all right here?" Joyce asked me. "We'll lock the door behind us. Don't let anyone in."

Did she think I was crazy or something? And yet she said the same thing to me every time she left me at home.

Actually I loved being at Margot's house when they were gone at night. Aside from my runs on the beach every morning, these were the only times I was away from Joyce. I went to the refrigerator and poured myself a glass of lemonade. Margot always had some in a glass pitcher with mint and real lemon slices in it. There were lots of things like that which made living here nice.

Margot's son still hadn't come for the weekend and he hardly ever called her either, even though he was just at Santa Cruz, five or six hours away. Boy, if Margot were my mother, I'd want to come home sometimes, that was for sure! But maybe that was what happened when you gave your kids a lot of freedom.

I took out my crescent moon earrings and went into

the bathroom to put them on. Now I could really study how they looked on me. I got a barrette and put my hair up. The curve of the moons seemed to frame my face, and whenever I moved, the stars hanging down swung and tinkled against my neck. These were the most beautiful earrings I'd ever seen.

Someday when I was grown up, I could wear them whenever I wanted, but at least now I could put them on sometimes, at school and other places where Joyce wouldn't see them. I still remembered how mad she'd been in Westwood when I asked her to look at them in Lionel's store. At the time I thought it was because of Lionel, but with Joyce you never could be sure.

The best place for the earrings was in my chest. That was my most hidden place and I had a key for it. I took out my jewelry box and felt below the black velvet bottom. The key was right where I'd left it.

My chest was like a miniature sea captain's chest with a curved top and metal bands and hinges. Joyce had given it to me for my tenth birthday, I think. The key turned easily in the lock and I opened it up.

In the chest, right next to my sunset pictures, I saw two thick stacks of money held together with rubber bands. Hundred-dollar bills were on top, and when I unfastened the stacks and counted them, they were all hundred-dollar bills. I counted each stack twice to be sure of what I was doing, but it came out the same way both times: $16,200 in that chest and Joyce must have hidden it there.

My arms and legs broke out in goose bumps and I felt myself start to tremble. Where had she gotten the money? It terrified me even to imagine it. But I think I was even more scared that Joyce would come into the room suddenly and catch me. Even though it was my chest, I felt like I shouldn't be snooping in it.

I locked up the chest again and quickly left our room. I still had the crescent earrings in my hand. There seemed to be no safe place now to hide them, nowhere they wouldn't be found. In desperation I ran into Margot's room and opened her closet. Piled on a shelf on top were several shoe boxes. I pulled one out at random and stuck the earrings under the lid. "Nickels," it said. I'd have to remember that.

It was the weirdest thing. From the time I'd found the money, I'd been acting to myself like a person in a movie who was committing a crime. I was hurrying and looking over my shoulder every minute, trying to cover my tracks. And yet *I hadn't done anything.*

I hardly slept that night. Joyce and Margot came in at about two and I heard Joyce stumbling around our room as she got undressed in the dark. I remember the sky turning paler and the birds piping up in the trees outside our windows, and finally it was five o'clock and I could get out of bed.

My mind was so busy, it was humming. For a long time I think I'd had questions about how we were living. Though I wasn't sure exactly what Joyce earned in her different jobs, I knew for example that a waitress made hardly any salary besides tips. And now of course she wasn't working at all.

It was a misty morning outside and the beach was almost empty. You could barely see ten feet in front of you. I walked along in the wet sand next to the ocean, trying to figure out when the money in the chest might have come into our lives. To me the scary part was that there could have once been more, a lot more—I had no idea.

I never planned to ask Joyce about it either, not with the way things had been going between us the last six months or so. Instead we'd just go on like we were, pretending that she was a normal mother and I was happy, pretending that we were close. $16,200 in my chest? What $16,200? What chest for that matter? See, it would be easy. Just one more lie added to the others.

When I thought like this, my heart felt like a lump frozen inside me. Maybe if Artie were here, I could cry in his arms again and not be so alone. But Artie was on his way back to Fresno already. He said his parents were going to leave at dawn so they wouldn't have to drive when the sun was hot. I didn't even know how to reach him in Fresno. Heck, I didn't know his last name!

When I walked up to the Santa Monica pier, all the usual sad types of people were sitting on benches, staring at the sea. Some of them might have been waiting for the bus that came along the beach every morning, passing out food for the homeless. I suddenly remembered how excited I'd been the first night we'd come to Venice. Not anymore. Now the whole place seemed sad and shabby to me and I saw that people were hungry.

It was probably time to go back to Margot's. I walked a long way and I thought Joyce would be awake by now. Sure enough, when I got to the street, she was hanging over the garden gate, looking up and down for me. "Oh, there you are," she said. "I was wondering."

Joyce used to have a spooky way of knowing if I was hiding something from her. "What's wrong, Nina?" she'd ask after I'd gotten a D on a test at school or had some kids be mean to me. She'd ask it the minute I'd walk in the door even though I'd walk in smiling. Of course that was when I was younger, probably up to about ten. "Have you had breakfast yet?" was all she said now. "Do you want some cold cereal?"

"I think I'll change into my bathing suit. We're going to the beach today, aren't we?"

"As soon as you're ready," said Joyce.

Actually, like a thief returning to the scene of the crime, I wanted to go back into our room and look at the money in the chest one more time. As soon as I saw that Joyce hadn't followed me, I went to take the key out of my jewelry box. My hands were shaking, she could come in at any moment, but I was driven to do this anyway. I lifted up the black velvet bottom and felt all over, but nothing was there. The key to the chest was gone.

I heard Joyce's footsteps out in the hall. "I forgot my bathing cap," she said. "Have you seen it lately, Nina?"

"I think it's on the hook in the bathroom." I was still holding my jewelry box with the top open, but neither of us acknowledged that.

16 The next day, in the middle of the afternoon, there was a knock at the door. Margot was out somewhere and Joyce and I saw two middle-aged men dressed in business suits. They were standing on the porch, not talking to each other, just waiting.

"Nina," said Joyce quietly. "I want you to go into our room. Close the door and just stay in there until I tell you to come out."

"What? Why?"

"Don't argue with me. Just do as I say."

I got up, but instead of going into our bedroom, I went into Margot's, which was right behind the living room.

"Yes?" said Joyce, opening the door.

There was a silence, as if something were changing

hands, papers or money or something. Then I heard a man's polite voice. "Good afternoon, ma'am. We're looking for a woman by the name of Georgia Halloran. We had some information she might live at this address."

"I'm sorry. I can't help you," Joyce said.

"Your name, ma'am?"

"Joyce Lewis."

"Does anyone else live here?" Now the other man was talking. I could tell because his voice was different, louder.

"Just my roommate. She's not home right now."

"And her name is?"

"Margot Rose."

Joyce had nerve, I thought. I'd been right in the living room when these men had come to the door. They could easily have seen me. It didn't really occur to me at the time to wonder why she hadn't just said she had a daughter.

"I'm sorry to have to ask you this, ma'am, but we'll need to see some proof of your identity."

"Will my passport be okay?" said Joyce.

"That'll be fine." Joyce's footsteps crossed the room and again there was silence as if something were being shown or looked at. Then the men spoke to each other, but I couldn't quite make out what they were saying. It was more of a murmur than actual words.

I heard the front door swing open. "Sorry to have bothered you, Mrs. Lewis," said one of the men.

She didn't answer him. The door slammed. I realized I'd been holding my breath.

"Goddammit," Joyce swore softly. "Goddammit to hell."

When I came back into the front of the house, she was sitting on a stool in the kitchen, not doing anything, just staring into space. "Do you know Margot's plans for tonight?" she asked me.

"I think she said she'd be back at around ten. She was working and going out to dinner with someone."

"Good," said Joyce. "We're going to be leaving here tonight and I want to be sure we're gone by the time she comes back."

"What?" All my anger and pain that I'd been putting aside as useless came rushing over me. I felt crazy with anger. "You told me we could stay!" I yelled. "You promised me!"

"Keep your voice down," said Joyce. She walked over and closed the kitchen window. "Don't you think you're a little old to throw a tantrum?"

I ran out of the kitchen. I was actually going to run out of the house but I remembered what Artie had said about how I ran away whenever things got bad. Okay, I wasn't going to do it this time, I decided.

So I made myself slow down. I went into the bathroom and looked at myself in the mirror and washed my face and hands with cold water. My face was tan and the California sun had turned my hair lighter. But I was seeing this from an enormous distance, as if the person I was looking at were somebody else.

Joyce was in our room, already pulling boxes and suitcases out of the closet. "We're going to need more boxes," she said, not even looking up. "You'll have to go to the liquor store on Washington Street and get some."

I let a moment or two pass and then I said, "Who were those men who came here just now? Were they from the police?"

Joyce put down the clothing she was holding and slowly got to her feet. "Well, yes," she said. "As a matter of fact, they were."

"What did they want?"

At first I thought she wasn't going to answer, but something must have made her change her mind. "They were looking for a woman named Georgia Halloran."

"Georgia Halloran is you, isn't she?"

As soon as I said these words, it was as if I'd always known them, as if I'd been *born* knowing that Joyce and Georgia Halloran were the same person. In the silence of the room, a chill went through my body, maybe like what people say happens when you walk over someone's grave.

Joyce didn't even try to deny it.

"But I don't understand. *Why* did you change your name?" I heard my own voice sounding shaky and full of tears, and Joyce came over and put her arm around me. Silky was in the room with us and she must have decided I needed comforting too, because she began licking my bare legs. "Yuck, Silky. Cut it out," I said.

"Can we talk about this later, Nina? We've got a lot to do to get out of here."

"I want to see Margot before we leave. I want to say good-bye to her," I said stubbornly.

"Don't you think I'd like that too? But it's not just a question of saying good-bye. I don't want Margot to have to tell lies on our behalf. This way she can just say, 'They were gone when I got home. I didn't know they were leaving. I have no idea where they went.' And it'll be true."

All the time she was talking, Joyce was emptying her bureau drawers into one of her suitcases. Now I pulled mine out from the closet and started to do the same.

"What about those boxes I asked you about?"

"I'll get them now." I had the clear feeling Joyce didn't want to leave the house. She might even be afraid the police would be watching it. I wanted to ask her what she'd done wrong, I wanted to ask her about the money in the chest; there were other things I wanted to ask her too. But I figured we had a long trip ahead of us in the van and I'd have her pinned down for days on end, right next to me in the driver's seat.

Before I left the house, I went into Margot's room and took my crescent moon earrings out of the Nickels shoe box. Compared to all that had just happened, anything that Joyce might have thought about them or not seemed completely minor.

I walked down our little narrow street and realized I was probably seeing the sights of Venice for the last time. There were some of our neighbors—the fat man who always walked by reading his newspaper, the Indian woman in her printed sari who lived across the street, the mother with two blonde twins, she had long hair and bare feet and looked about eighteen to me. I'd come to recognize all these people now, and they didn't seem nearly so strange as they had when we'd first moved here.

But what was I going to do about saying good-bye to Artie? He'd be expecting me on Saturday at the lifeguard station and I'd just never come. I could picture him there, leaning against one of the poles and skipping stones into the water, waiting and waiting for hours. There had to be some way to get a message to him.

Margot. Joyce wouldn't like it, but she wouldn't have to know about it either. I could call Margot collect while we were on the road. Today was only Tuesday. Maybe I could get Joyce to stay over in a motel one night before the weekend so that I could use the phone.

She brought it up. I didn't even have to ask. We were driving through Colorado, we'd just come out of the Rockies and it was about four in the afternoon. The highway signs said *Pueblo*. "This looks like a good-sized town coming up," said Joyce. "What do you say we shop here for some things we need and stay overnight at a motel."

We were on our way to New York City, she'd told me. She wanted to get as far from Venice as possible, a continent away. It was that simple. At another time, even a year ago, I would have been excited. New York City, the Big Apple! But now everything we were doing had a feeling of desperation about it, like we were being pushed faster and faster.

"Are we running away?" I'd asked her the night before when we'd left Venice. We'd thrown all our stuff in the van and gotten out of the house only half an hour before Margot was supposed to come back. Joyce was driving like the police really *were* after her. Five miles over the speed limit and driving all night.

Instead of answering me, Joyce asked another questions. This was typical of her at the time. "Why do you think we'd be running away?"

"Is it the money?" I asked. "The money in my chest?"

Willie Nelson was playing on our tape deck. "Blue Skies smiling at me. Nothing but Blue Skies do I see." I remember the sky actually was beginning to turn blue, high above the scrubby Nevada desert.

"I *thought* you'd found that," said Joyce. "The chest seemed like a good place for it. Because of the lock, I mean."

"But where did you get $16,200?" I forced myself to go on. "Did you steal it? Is that why you changed your name?"

Joyce's eyes were fixed on the road and I couldn't tell much from her face. "I wanted to protect you, that's all. I wanted you to grow up without having to worry about what I'd done or what was going to happen. If we hadn't gone to Venice, everything would still be fine too. We were getting along, right? Our life wasn't bad. But I had to show you Venice. Venice, big fucking deal! Why do I always do that? Why do I always mess things up in the end?"

She pulled in to a rest stop. It was really only a wide spot on the road with overflowing trash barrels. Then she turned off the ignition and threw herself onto the steering wheel like she was throwing herself into someone's arms. Her shoulders shook and I realized she was crying. I'd never seen Joyce cry before. Never.

I was terrified. I remembered myself as a little child, waking up in the night. As soon as I called for Joyce, she'd be there. No danger could touch me. But if Joyce was crying now, that meant neither of us was safe. I waited for her to stop and looked out through the rearview mirror. But it was all right. The road behind us was empty. I didn't see a single car.

In Pueblo we found a motel called a TraveLodge; they have them all across the West. Our room was okay but whoever was staying there before us must have smoked a lot. There was an air conditioner humming when we walked in, but the place still stank. The first thing Joyce did was to pull back the drapes and open the windows. She left the air conditioner on too. "We're paying for it, aren't we?" she said.

We both took showers and we ate in the motel's coffee shop. Then we strolled down the wide main street of the town, looking for an open drugstore. Joyce wanted to buy some dye to do her hair. The roots were really beginning to show. They used to be just brown, but I could see she had a lot of gray coming in now too.

It always amazes me how many hair and skin products there are in drugstores. Row after row, each one slightly different and making different promises. Sometimes I can feel myself getting nervous as I try to choose. But Joyce seemed to know just what she wanted. "Born Blonde by Clairol," she said. "We can both be blondes."

"Not me," I said. "No way." I was attached to how I looked. I was a redhead. That was a really strong part of my personality. It wasn't like having brown or blonde hair.

Joyce took the dye up to the counter along with a rubber sheet and a big package of M&M's and paid for them without saying a word. But once we were back in our room, she told me she was worried about the police finding us. "I'm not asking you to be someone you're not," she said. "It's probably dumb of me, but

I keep looking over my shoulder. This way if we're blondes, they'll be that much less likely to find us."

She was hurrying around, getting bowls out of the van and setting up the different lotions and bottles of dye on the bathroom counter. I was to go first. She dyed one strand of my hair just to see if it would work. Then she draped the rubber sheet around me and made me sit on the toilet. I hated having to do this, hated bowing my head while Joyce dabbed at the roots of my hair and the cold chemical-smelling stuff dripped down my neck. But how could I refuse?

Even though we both used the same dye and timed it the same, my hair came out much lighter than Joyce's. To me, that paleness didn't go with my face at all. I didn't even want to look in the mirror. I felt like something really damaging had happened to me, like I'd been hurt or wounded in some way. I tried to tell myself it was only hair. Hair grows half an inch a month. Would Joyce feel we were safe in six months? In ninth months? In a year?

I was planning to call Margot after Joyce was asleep, but at ten o'clock, when she was already in her night-gown, she asked me to go walk Silky. They don't allow dogs in the TraveLodge, they never do in motels. Silky was glad to see me and we had a nice walk in the short grass by the roadside. Then I went back into the lobby and called Margot.

I could hear the long-distance wires humming as the operator put the call through. "I have a collect call from Nina Lewis. Will you accept the charges?"

"Nina! Are you all right? I've been so worried about you!" As soon as I heard Margot's voice, everything seemed to come back to normal, or at least it settled down a little.

"Sure, I'm fine, it's just that we had to leave suddenly. I'm sorry we couldn't say good-bye."

"Where are you calling from?"

"We're in Colorado." I had the idea I shouldn't be too specific about where we were, even with Margot. A memory of her, of how friendly and relaxed she'd always been, made me feel guilty. But I had to trust what Joyce said right now.

"Listen, Margot, can you do me a favor? It's about Artie. My friend who you met?"

"Of course."

"I was supposed to meet him on Saturday at the lifeguard station. That's what we always do every Saturday. But we're not coming back there. At least not for a while."

"Do you want me to meet him instead? I could say good-bye for you."

"Yes, but it's at five in the morning."

"I can do that. I'll just set my alarm." She rushed on. "I'm so glad you called, Nina. I can't tell you. It was so strange the night you and Joyce left. At first I felt furious, like how could they do this to me after I let them come and live here and I didn't even know them. But then I realized something must be wrong or you never would have done it. I won't ask you to say what it is unless you want to. What about Joyce? Is she there? Does she want to talk to me?"

"No, she's sleeping. She was really tired. But she sends her love." I was beginning to get nervous. If too much time passed, Joyce might come looking for me. "Listen, Margot, I have to go now."

"Where are you going to be staying?" she asked.

"I think New York. But I'm not really sure. Somewhere around the city anyway. Maybe New Jersey. Are you sure you don't mind about Artie?"

"Five on Saturday at the lifeguard station. I'll be there."

"Great. Thanks, Margot. We'll call you later."

Of course it was a lie. We never would. When I hung up the phone and walked back through the hotel lobby, I felt like my final link to the past had been broken.

✔ Part Four

Brooklyn, New York

17 I'll tell you, it was hot. More than the dirt or the smell or the feeling of danger everywhere, that was what surprised me most about New York.

We decided to live in the borough of Brooklyn. When Joyce was a kid, she'd been a fan of the Brooklyn Dodgers, a baseball team that doesn't even exist anymore. It was a weird reason to choose a place to live but better than nothing, I guess. The truth is, neither of us really knew what we were doing. From the moment the police had come to Margot's door, it felt like all the rules for our life had changed.

"If anyone ever asks you if you're Nina Lewis, I want you to say you're not," Joyce told me the day we arrived in New York.

I wasn't even surprised. "Who do you want me to be?"

"That's up to you," said Joyce. "You decide."

We were walking with Silky on a street next to Prospect Park. As soon as we'd gotten into Brooklyn and felt the waves of heat coming up from the cement streets, Joyce had asked a Black woman on the sidewalk where a big park was. "Prospect Park. That's the biggest one we got," said the woman. "Go straight down Flatbush till you come to the monument."

"Where's Flatbush?" asked Joyce.

The woman looked at Joyce in a pitying way, as if Joyce were retarded or something. "Flatbush Avenue. This is it," she said. "You're on it."

When we got to the park it was a little better, or at least it was cooler. "We have to find an apartment near here," said Joyce. "I don't care how much it costs. We'll just go in to a real estate agent and take whatever they have."

That's when she said the remark about changing my name. We sat down on a park bench, each looking off in a different direction. The trees above us barely moved and the sky was overcast and gritty. I thought about my name. If I wasn't Nina Lewis, was I really Nina Halloran? Who would I be next? Did it even matter?

In the street, cars were honking, dogs were barking, and people were shouting at one another. But no one talked to us or looked at us. Maybe this is why Joyce wanted to come to New York. You could be right in front of people, but they wouldn't even see you. It was the weirdest thing.

"Have you thought of a last name? My mind's a blank," said Joyce. Her face was tired and the yellow dye had turned her hair stiff as straw. In her pleated Bermuda shorts and tube top, she didn't look like my pretty mother at all, but like an older woman who was trying to look young. It made me embarrassed for her, and yet I felt sorry for her at the same time.

"How about Harris?" I offered.

"Too much like Lewis."

"Gordon?" I was thinking of Sam.

"No. Think of something more unusual."

"Carpenter."

"Good, that'll do. Carpenter. I'll be Judy Carpenter. What about you?"

I thought about all the friends I'd ever had. But there wasn't really one of them I wanted to name myself after. "Can I be Margot?" I asked.

"I guess so," said Joyce. "At least I'm used to that name." She took out her comb and compact from her purse and combed her hair. "We better get to a real estate agent. I don't want to leave the van out on the street. If worse comes to worse, we can always stay in a hotel for a while."

It seems like people in New York City have to be either very rich or very poor to live here. The apartment we finally got cost *$700 a month*. But what was even more amazing to me was that the real estate agent kept calling it a bargain. She was a fat, enthusiastic woman. "You won't find garden apartments like this every day, believe me, Mrs. Carpenter."

"We believe you," said Joyce wearily. It was true. We'd looked at about twenty apartments and all of them cost more than the one we finally rented. It did have a little garden of its own though, with a tiny grape arbor in the back and two red rose bushes.

All the houses in this part of Brooklyn were called brownstones because of the kind of stone they were made of. They were attached to one another in a row, and the gardens in back were separated by chain-link fences. As Joyce and the real estate agent were going over some details about the rental (Joyce had actually come up with references for Judy Carpenter—don't ask me how), I wandered out into the garden.

It was a quieter, calmer world back here. You could hear people's televisions and the hum of air conditioners. You could hear the voices of children playing and a singer in one of the apartments who was practicing scales. "Do re mi fa sol la ti do," she sang over and over. I wondered if I would ever hear her sing a real song.

Was New York going to be a good place for us to hide? Were we going to be able to stay here? If so, I could get used to it. I had already checked out the street scene on this block. There were at least two groups of kids my age, both boys and girls, fooling around on the high front stoops of the brownstones. They looked a little tough and some of them were Black and Spanish, but I thought I could handle that all right. None of them had been around as much as me, that was for sure!

It wasn't that I liked my life, but you have to take the good with the bad. I had seen a lot and done a lot and now all those experiences were part of me. They were the weapons I had to meet the world with.

All the time I was thinking this, I was sitting on some rickety steps leading down to the garden from the back door of the apartment we'd rented. Suddenly I heard the back door of the next house slam. An old man and a little girl came out and stared at me without even trying to disguise it. I put my hands on my head. I was worried about my blonde hair. It was so blonde compared to how they looked.

The old man was brown and thin, but strong-looking too. He wore a straw hat with a narrow brim and I thought he was Spanish or Mexican. The little girl with him was probably his granddaughter. She had on gold earrings even though she was only about six.

"Hi. What's your name?" she asked.

This was it, the first time I had to say I was someone else. I had the feeling that the girl and the old man weren't going to believe me, or that they'd argue with me about it and give me a hard time. It was really stupid though, because how were they supposed to know who I was? Even if I said my name was Molly

Ringwald (she's my favorite actress), they'd probably just say, "That's nice. Glad to meet you."

I got up and walked over to the chain-link fence. "Margot Carpenter," I said. "What's yours?"

"Laurel Mendenez. This is my grandfather. He don't speak English though."

The old man smiled at me and stuck out his hand as if he knew that an introduction had been made. He had a very kind and handsome face. "Good day, miss," he said in perfect English.

"Is that you, Margot?" called Joyce. "Who are you talking to? It's time to go. We're leaving now."

I shook the old man's hand. "Glad to meet you," I said. "We're leaving now."

"When'll you come back?" Laurel asked.

"Tomorrow. We're moving in here."

Joyce came outside and stood next to me but I didn't introduce her to them or say she was my mother. I didn't feel like it, that's all.

The heat didn't let up. It was almost 100 every day and even the commentators on the radio said that it was the worst heat wave New York had had in twenty years. "Great," said Joyce. "It would have to happen just when we moved here. What else is new?"

But I didn't mind. I'd gotten to know not only Laurel and Mr. Mendenez but the other people who lived next door to us too. There were three dark, good-looking boys who were Laurel's cousins, and her mother and two aunts. No men except the grandfather lived in the house, and Laurel was the only girl. The boys were always busy, hosing down the backyard or walking Rex, their Great Dane, out on the street, but they were friendly when I saw them. Laurel told me two of them went to high school at John Jay. This school was only eight blocks from us and it was where I'd be going too, in the fall.

Laurel was pretty cool. She was the pet of the family and she knew a whole lot for a little kid who was only six. She'd come out back first thing every morning and call to me, "Margot, are you there?" I'd probably be eating my cereal by then and I'd take it outside. Then she'd squeeze through a gap in the fence and come sit beside me. She'd tell me about everyone in her family, what their likes and dislikes were, and what her mother and aunts did for a living. I think she was lonely for other girls to talk to. I certainly was.

I'd made a few tries at meeting the kids closer to my age who were on the street, but Joyce wasn't happy about it. Every time I was beginning to talk to someone or find out what was going on, I'd hear Joyce's voice, "Margot, could you come in here for a minute?" She would never actually forbid me to make friends with anyone but there was always some reason I had to come in.

The kids on the street didn't even seem to *have* parents. They seemed to run their own lives completely. You could hear them with their tape decks

(but here they called them boxes) until two o'clock
in the morning, and no one ever called them inside
or came looking for them. They rode their bikes on
the sidewalk or cruised up and down on skateboards,
but it was all in a casual way, as if they were just
passing the long summer days.

Most of the time Joyce and I stayed in the apartment
or else she had me run errands for her. It wasn't that
she *never* went out, it's just that she preferred to let
me do things. I soon got to know the location of all
the shops. In Brooklyn there weren't many supermar-
kets. You had to go from shop to shop—one for bread,
another for fruits and vegetables, another for meat.
For small things like toilet paper or a carton of milk
we went to the bodega, a Spanish grocery store on our
corner.

Two things made August better. I bought a shopping
cart and I found out where the library was. I'd started
reading books again, almost a book a day. I'd gotten
out of the habit the past few years, but now I felt that
books were just what I needed. I mainly took out
mysteries. I liked to see how the detectives in them
solved their crimes. My own life seemed like a mystery,
too, but one without a beginning or end.

In a way my best hope was that nothing more would
happen to us. If it did, I felt sure it would be something
bad. Every time I saw a policeman on the street, my
heart would start racing and I'd have to tell myself to
keep walking along as if I were just ordinary—an or-

dinary blonde thirteen-year-old girl doing the shopping for her mother.

I had tried to ask Joyce a few more times why the police had come looking for her, but she still wouldn't say much about it or tell me why she'd changed her name. There were always murders in the mysteries I read but I was positive Joyce could never have done anything like that.

"Did you steal the money in my chest?" I asked her straight out as we were going to bed one night.

"Yes," she said, "I did. I did steal it. Now are you satisfied?"

The way she answered didn't sound real, but I was no detective. Joyce was my mother and I was her daughter and I had no idea what to do.

For weeks I'd been pleading with Joyce to take me to the beach, and finally the day after I asked about the money, she said she would. We were only about ten miles from the Atlantic Ocean. Strange as it seems, New York is a city surrounded by water. At night when it was quiet, you could hear foghorns in the harbor. I couldn't wait to run near the ocean again!

"Can we take Laurel with us?" I asked. Laurel hardly ever got to go anywhere. Her family gave the boys a lot of freedom, but for some reason they expected her to stay around the house. She'd never even been to Prospect Park.

"It's a nice idea, kiddo, but what if something should

happen? No, I don't think we better." Joyce was getting changed and packing the straw beach bag. We
had to go pick up the van. It had been parked in a
garage two blocks away ever since we'd moved to our
apartment.

We didn't really know how to get to the beach, but
the guy who worked in the garage said we should take
the Belt Parkway to Riis Park. The road ran along the
edge of the city and it was good for once to be outside
the buildings and the crowded narrow streets. On the
other side of the road, New York Bay sparkled and
boats were sailing on the water.

Since it was Tuesday and we'd started in the afternoon, the beach wasn't all that crowded by the time
we got there. It was a much wider beach than in
Venice, with sand dunes and beach grass in back. It
was fun to watch the people. On one side of us a boy
was burying his girlfriend in sand up to her neck, and
on the other side of us four middle-aged people in red
beach chairs were playing cards like they were at home
in their living room.

That day Joyce and I had a wonderful time together.
The waves were gentle swells and we lay on them on
our backs, rising and falling under the hot blue sky.
By the time we came out of the water, we were so
relaxed we could hardly even speak.

Finally at eight when the beach was closing, Joyce
said, "What do you say we stop somewhere for dinner?
Maybe we can get some seafood."

"Sure. Why not?"

We unrolled all the windows of the van and the evening breeze cooled us as we drove along. I thought of so many other occasions like this, with Joyce and me driving along, halfway between two new places, feeling both calm and expectant. What a team we made sometimes.

18

It was on the way back from dinner that the policeman stopped us. We'd eaten at a big seafood restaurant in Rockaway and were trying to find our way back to the parkway through the suburban streets when we suddenly heard the siren and saw a blue light flashing behind us.

"Get in the back of the van, quick! Cover yourself with the beach blanket!" Joyce sounded absolutely terrified.

I climbed over the seat and stretched out flat against the side of the van, putting the blanket over my face and grabbing the bottom with my toes. It was only a thin cotton blanket. If they tried to find me, they would. I just hoped they wouldn't be looking.

Joyce slowed down and pulled the van to the side of the road. It seemed like I lay there forever, but it was probably only a minute or so before the policeman walked over. The blue light of his patrol car swept the van but he'd turned the siren off.

"Evening, ma'am. I'll need to see your license and registration."

I heard Joyce fumbling through her bag and then a click as she opened the glove compartment.

The policeman must have gone back to his car, either that or he was awfully quiet. "Are you okay?" Joyce whispered.

"I'm fine, don't worry."

More time went by. Then footsteps came back, crunching in the gravel by the side of the road. "Thanks very much, ma'am. You can put these away now."

"Would you mind telling me what this is all about, officer?" It was the first time Joyce had actually spoken to the policeman. "Here I am on my way back from a nice day at the beach and you stop me with no explanation for almost ten minutes?"

"You've got a taillight out. That means you have up to five days to get it repaired. If you don't and we catch you, it carries a fifty-dollar fine."

Good. Then we hadn't been caught. A taillight. That was nothing.

"You're pretty far from Utah, Mrs. Lawrence. Or is it Miss?" the policeman went on.

"Miss."

My feeling of relief vanished. Lawrence? Who was

Miss Lawrence? Of course it was Joyce, Joyce with still another name. It had to be.

"How long will you be in New York State, Miss Lawrence?" The policeman's voice sounded regular, almost conversational by now.

"Oh, just a few more days. I came to Brooklyn to visit my mother."

"Well, have a nice trip home. And see that you get that taillight fixed. Some states don't take to broken taillights as kindly as we do in New York."

"I will. Thanks for the warning."

The siren sounded once more, a short high blast, and then the policeman drove away. He accelerated so fast, his tires squealed. Probably he was showing off for Joyce. "Stay under there a little longer," she said to me. "Just in case."

But I ignored her and climbed back to the front seat. Now I was really mad at Joyce. With her phony names and her secrets, I felt like she was betraying me not just once, but over and over again. I put the radio on. Joyce had the dial on WNEW, an AM station that plays slow jazz at night, but I turned it to the loudest rock and roll music I could find.

"What's the matter, Nina?" Joyce looked over at me and almost swerved into the curb.

"I don't want you to keep doing this to me. That's all."

"Doing what?" asked Joyce. "Isn't it enough I just

got stopped by the police? What am I doing to you?"

"It's not right," I said. "I agree to everything you want. I dye my hair and change my name just because you say to. And all our lives we've moved every time you said it was time to move. Well, I'm not a little kid anymore—I understand lots of things."

"I know you're not. You've always been very grown-up for your age."

I could tell I was making her nervous. "Don't you trust me?" I said. "The least you can do is let me know who these different people are. Georgia Halloran and Joyce Lewis. And now I find out about Lawrence. Who is that? Who is she?"

Joyce turned the radio way down and I heard her sigh. "Lorraine Lawrence. That's the name I use to register the car and when I need to give a Social Security number at a job. Things like that."

"Is it an alias?"

"Yes."

"So that means you have four different names, counting Judy Carpenter?"

"Yes."

"Do you have any more?"

"No. That's it."

We were on the Belt Parkway now, streaming back to Brooklyn with all the other cars and vans and taxis. For some reason I believed Joyce. I knew she was telling the truth.

Something woke me up. Outside on the street a dog barked. Silky was by my side and she growled softly. I heard a key turn in the lock. "Joyce, wake up," I whispered, tiptoeing into her room. But she wasn't there. Her bed hadn't even been slept in.

The light from the hallway illuminated the room for an instant, but it was long enough for me to see that the person coming in was Joyce. I sat down on the mattress in her room, realizing only then how frightened I'd been. "Where were you?" I said. "You scared me."

She walked over to the windows and pulled down the shades. Then she turned on a light. Despite the heat she was wearing blue jeans and a long-sleeved shirt. A silk scarf covered her hair. "What time is it?" she asked.

"It must be six in the morning." I checked my alarm clock. "It's twenty to six," I said.

"I ditched the van," said Joyce. "I took the license plates off and ditched it." She went into the kitchen and I followed her. We sat at the table, looking into the back garden. The sky was beginning to get light. "Do you want some tea?" she said.

"I'll do it." I put the kettle on to boil and waited for her to say more. It was funny, but it seemed like the events of the past twelve hours—the policeman stopping us and now this—had made us more like equals than we'd ever been before. Or maybe Joyce was just too frightened to stay quiet.

She told me how she'd driven the van up into Connecticut, to a town called Norwalk, and abandoned it under a big highway. Nobody had seen her as she'd unscrewed the license plates and put them in a shopping bag. She'd waited an hour for a train and then she'd stood between the cars and heaved the license plates over a bank halfway between Connecticut and New York City.

When she'd gotten into Grand Central Station in Manhattan, Joyce said she was too nervous to take the subway to Brooklyn, so she'd taken a cab. "It's dangerous in Manhattan at that hour," she told me. "You should always take a cab home if it's after ten o'clock at night."

I made the tea and set it in front of Joyce but she didn't even seem to notice. She'd taken off her scarf and kept running her fingers through her hair. It was so dry and coarse from the dye and the saltwater that it stood up in spikes all around her head. "You look like a real punker," I said. Actually without any makeup and with the dark circles under her eyes, she looked a lot worse than that.

"I must look awful," said Joyce, taking her compact out of her purse.

"No, you look fine," I said. "What about your driver's license? Did you throw that out too?"

She covered her mouth with her hand. "My driver's license! I didn't even think of it."

I was very curious to see this license. Joyce had

taught me from a really young age not to ever go in her purse. If I wanted money, even a quarter, I'd have to hand her her purse and then she'd take out her wallet and give me the money. I'd thought all parents were like that. I still couldn't believe she had papers saying she was somebody else, a woman named Lorraine Lawrence.

She showed me a small plastic card. "What should I do with it?" she asked.

All the information was there. Lawrence, Lorraine, it said, 490 West 300 North, Logan, Utah 84321. Eyes, brown. Hair, red. And there was a picture of Joyce, smiling merrily in her winter jacket.

"Cut it up, I guess."

"Of course, cut it up. You're right," said Joyce.

By this time the sun was shining through the window. I got out the orange juice and put four pieces of bread in the oven to toast. Then I handed Joyce a scissors.

Joyce hadn't been going out much, but after that night she stopped completely. I was put in charge of everything concerning the outside world. I didn't mind. It was me who figured out when errands needed to be done and it was me who did them. Joyce's only part was in giving me the money.

One day when I was at the Laundromat doing the wash, I saw a sign on a bulletin board announcing the opening of school. It listed what shots were needed

and said no child would be allowed to go to school
without them. I guess it was mainly for kids who'd be
starting kindergarten, but it made me realize that we
should make sure my records were in order. It was
already September 2, and school began the day after
Labor Day.

This was a really nice Laundromat, and believe me,
I've been in plenty of them nationwide. As I was
copying the information off the sign, a woman who'd
been waiting for her wash came and stood next to me.
"Are you starting school next week, or is it for somebody else?"

"No, me."

"What school will you be going to?"

"John Jay. It's on Seventh Avenue."

"Oh, that's where my daughter goes. What grade
are you going into?"

"Ninth."

"Jan too. You should meet her sometime."

I took a closer look at this woman. She was actually
one of the few people who'd been friendly to me in
Brooklyn. The only other time anyone even talked to
me was in the park, but that was just because I had
Silky with me and they were dog owners too. For
example, they never even asked me my name, only
Silky's, and I only knew the names of their dogs.

"My name's Ruth Boardman. Aren't those your ma-
chines that just stopped?"

We walked over to the two dryers I was using and

she helped me take out my laundry and fold it on one of the long tables they had. The heat from the dryers was still in the clothes but the Laundromat was air-conditioned, so it wasn't that bad.

While we folded, we talked. Mrs. Boardman was a soft-looking woman with curly light brown hair and a round face. What I liked about her right away was that she seemed plain. She didn't talk fast or wise the way lots of people do in New York.

"Are you from here?" I asked her to keep the conversation going.

"No, I grew up in Vermont."

"Vermont! We used to live in Montpelier."

"I'm from Plainfield."

"That's really close!" I said, excited to think of the geography of a place I'd liked so much.

"Then you must have gone to the Montpelier middle school. Did you know Fred Jenks? I think he teaches science there, or maybe math. His father used to work on my parents' farm."

Nothing like this had happened to me before! I didn't know what to say or do. I thought of all Joyce's warnings—how I wasn't supposed to be in contact with anyone I knew in the past.

I glanced over at Mrs. Boardman and saw her staring at me. My face felt hot. I hoped I wasn't blushing.

"We moved to Utah when I was in fifth grade," I said. "I never went to the Montpelier middle school."

"For someone your age, it sounds like you've had

an interesting life. All that moving! I think Jan would really like to meet you. Why don't you give me your address? Or else you could go see her sometime. She's working at the Bagel Store. You know, near Prospect Place?"

"Okay, maybe I will." I ignored the part about giving my address. I certainly wasn't about to do that. And she didn't know my name either, so there was really no way she could find me. I hated having to be so suspicious. It made me feel like I was turning into Joyce. Here was this nice middle-aged woman helping me with my laundry, and I was acting like she was holding a knife to my throat!

"Thanks a lot," I told her as she held the door open so I could get my shopping cart through. "I really appreciate it."

"Look up Jan," she said. "I'll tell her you'll be coming by."

"Okay, thanks for everything." The humid air on the street prickled my skin but I was still glad to get out of there.

Those late summer days were hard with a feeling of always being locked up or trapped against my will. Our apartment made it worse, I think. It had only three rooms. Joyce slept in the front room, and the middle room, which was my bedroom, had no windows at all. I'd put up my sunset collage, but it hadn't really helped.

The real problem though was Joyce. She was nervous

and jumpy and she'd started to drink more at night.
I'd wake up, especially on the hotter nights, and hear
the radio on in the kitchen. There was a big armchair
that the last tenant had left and Joyce would be sitting
in the dark, with a bottle of scotch in front of her and
listening to a late-night jazz show on WNEW.

"Come to bed," I'd tell her. "Get some sleep."

She'd reach out for my hands, groping for them in
the dark. "Don't worry, Nina. We're going to be just
fine."

"I know that," I'd say. "But you should still get some
sleep."

I'd told her about school starting and I asked her to
give me my records. "If you don't want to come when
I register, I can do it myself," I said.

But on the Friday before Labor Day Joyce announced
that I wouldn't be going back to school. We were in
the garden eating supper. I'd brought the folding table
and chairs out so we could enjoy a little bit of breeze
and we were having a cold meal—ham and turkey and
macaroni salad from the deli.

I sat there like a character in a cartoon with my
fork poised halfway to my mouth. "What do you mean?
I can't go to school?"

"Just for now," said Joyce. "Just until I feel like we're
safe again."

"But when will that be? Nothing's happened since
that time we got stopped, and you yourself said that
was only because we were on Long Island. We're safe

here. I'm the one that's walking around and I'm sure
it's fine. Nobody pays any attention. A person could
get shot on the street and people would just walk
around him."

Joyce shrugged. "You'll only miss a few weeks. How
bad is that?"

I closed my eyes and felt a rush of despair, more
than I'd let myself feel or even know about since we'd
come to New York. No matter where we'd lived or
what else had been going on, Joyce had always sent
me to school. Education was really important to her.
She wanted me to go to college.

"If you don't feel safe here, we could go somewhere
else." I said. "I don't care, just as long as I can start
school."

Joyce started clearing the table. "Not now. I can't
handle it yet, Nina. There's so much to do. I've got
to get a driver's license in the first place and a new
vehicle. Do you think that's easy?"

"But are we going to move again or will we stay in
Brooklyn?"

I felt like I was pushing at her, coming at her with
all these questions when she was weak, but I was beginning to get scared that nothing was ever going to
change, that I was never going to go to high school,
but would be stuck forever with Joyce and my dark
room and my little round of errands.

She walked away and looked over the fence, into

the Mendenezes' yard. "Give me two weeks, then ask me again. Please."

"Will you tell me in two weeks?"

"I promise," said Joyce.

19 Maybe it was because she had hangovers, I don't know, but every morning Joyce slept until almost ten. I wasn't doing my running in New York. I'd tried it a few times in Prospect Park, but there were so many other people running, it was like being caught in a traffic jam. One of the things about running I loved most was the privacy, so forget that. Instead, while Joyce was asleep, I'd fallen into a routine of playing with Laurel in our garden.

It reminded me of my childhood. It really did. Or at least of the time we lived in Toronto and I had my friend Janice. I was close to Laurel's age then, about five or six, so I knew just how to play with Laurel, what she'd like to do best.

The grape arbor in back of our garden was covered with vines (and green grapes too) and it was like a leafy green room. We made miniature place mats from the grape leaves and used pebbles and seeds we found for cups and plates and food. We'd pretend to have tea. Silky would be there, and Laurel would bring out a few stuffed animals to be the other guests.

It sounds stupid, I know, but there was actually something comforting about it. Every day we'd set up the tea party the same way and spend an hour or two hidden away from the world. Usually what finally happened was that Joyce would wake up and come outside in her nightgown and I'd make Laurel go home. Nobody from her family came outside in *their* nightgowns.

"What do you want to play with that little girl for?" Joyce would say to me.

Who do you want me to play with? I thought, but I never said it out loud. Joyce was so frightened and strange right now that I automatically wanted to protect her. Some days she wouldn't get dressed at all, but would sit on her bed in the front room with the shades drawn, not even reading or knitting. "Come sit beside me," she'd say, and when I did, she'd take my hand and tell me stories of things we'd done together when I was little. It embarrassed me, but it made me sad too. Sometimes I'd have to turn my face away because I felt like crying.

During the time kids were at school, Joyce wouldn't let me go out except in the backyard. I guess she didn't want the police noticing us for that. But at three or three-fifteen when we heard the neighborhood kids laughing and calling to each other on their way home, I was allowed to take Silky for a walk to the park.

Finally in the second week of September the heat

broke, and it was like the city began to wake up. People moved faster and the air got clear and sunny. I loved being in the park those afternoons. But I missed school so much, especially when I saw teenagers, boys and girls walking together, or even a group of girls in their brand-new school clothes. It had been a long time since life had felt normal to me or I'd paid attention to things like that.

One day Silky and I stayed in the park longer than usual. We'd started out on a different path and we walked and walked until we came to a little lake. This was really something! A lake in New York City! There were rowboats and canoes and I saw two little Black boys fishing with their father. Probably the water was too polluted to eat the fish, but at least they were trying. I sat on a bench for a long time and watched as the father showed the boys how to thread worms onto the fishhooks and how to cast the lines. But when he turned and saw me, I quickly walked away.

It was almost seven by the time I got home. I decided to pick up a pizza on Seventh Avenue. Joyce didn't plan meals or cook anymore, so I could get whatever I wanted, but they had to make the pizza to order and it took a while. I ran the last three blocks. I didn't want her worrying about me.

To get to our apartment you have to go down a couple of steps and then unlock a big iron gate. I put the pizza down on the ground so I could use both hands, but the moment I touched the gate, it swung open by itself. "Joyce, I'm home now," I called. "Why didn't you lock the door?"

Silky barked just once, and at the exact moment I realized Joyce wasn't there, that she wasn't in the apartment at all—two men came toward me, walking out of the kitchen. They looked a lot like the last men, the ones who'd come to Margot's door in Venice, but this time I was seeing them up close and Joyce couldn't talk to them or keep them away from me.

"Don't be alarmed," one of them said. "We're here to help you."

"Is your name Nina Lewis?" The other man took out his wallet and opened it up. I saw his picture on a plastic card like Joyce's license. "Federal Bureau of Investigation," it said. "United States Department of Justice." Were they policemen or not? I didn't know.

My heart ached—it actually ached from terror. "Where's my mother?" I said.

"Is your name Nina Lewis?" the man with the plastic card repeated.

"No. Margot Carpenter."

"But that's only been since you and Joyce came to Brooklyn last month. Correct?"

What was I supposed to say? "If anyone asks, say you're Margot Carpenter," Joyce had told me, but she hadn't realized that the men would already know so much about us.

So I didn't answer at all. I stood there in the front

room of our apartment, knowing that on this day and at this moment my life was changing forever, while the noises outside went on as if it were any other day. The garbage truck passed by with its roller compacting the trash from a hundred, a thousand, apartments in New York City and all I could think was that it was a weird time for them to collect the garbage.

I must have swayed on my feet then because one of the men took my arm and led me over to Joyce's mattress. "Why don't you sit down?" he said. His voice wasn't harsh or mean and I thought they were probably sorry for me. But I was too scared to ask them another time where they had taken Joyce.

I sat and they continued standing, not asking me any more questions or talking to each other. It was like we were locked there endlessly, although probably it was only a minute or so until the doorbell rang. I don't think anyone had ever rung the doorbell before, it confused me until I realized what it was. "Probably Ruth Boardman," one of the men said and went to answer the door.

The name didn't register. Truthfully I didn't think about it. If these men—if they were policemen or from the FBI—were in our apartment, to me that meant anyone could come in.

But then I looked up and saw that I knew this person and she was the woman from the Laundromat. She was more dressed up than she'd been that day and she was carrying a pizza, holding it carefully away from her clothing. "Someone left this outside," she said. "Hello, Nina."

She smiled at me the way she had the first time, as if we were already friends. I wanted to close my eyes against that smile.

So she's a part of this too! I thought. It was like a net they'd been drawing tighter and tighter around us. Now I saw that Joyce had been right to be so frightened, but I wished she'd warned me better. At least she'd should have told me what to do if they came.

I couldn't run out the door. They would have stopped me, I was sure of that, so I turned over on my stomach and buried my face in the pillow on Joyce's bed. I could smell the shampoo she used and I felt the soft cotton pillowcase. I felt so ill, I wanted to both sob and throw up.

"Have you explained anything to her?" It was the woman's voice. Ruth Boardman's.

"Not yet," one of the men said, and I think they must have walked back into the kitchen, because I heard their voices whispering far away. I lay there for a long time, while the nausea grew and jumped from my stomach to my throat. Then I ran to the bathroom and threw up in the toilet again and again until there was nothing left inside me.

When I finally came out, only Ruth Boardman was still there, sitting at the kitchen table. The men had gone and it was quiet in the room. "Would you like a glass of water?" she asked me. "Sometimes it helps to drink water."

She ran water in the sink, holding her finger in the stream to see if it was cool.

"We keep ice water in the refrigerator," I said and I got the gallon jug out and poured myself a glass.

"So today you just came home from the park as usual and your mother was gone and two strange men were here? And then you saw me and realized we'd been watching you?"

I nodded.

"That must have been terrifying," she said. "You must want to know why."

I nodded again, feeling the nausea start up again and my throat start to ache. This was it, I thought, this was when she was going to answer all the questions. Now I was going to find out everything.

"Joyce is not your mother."

It was exactly like she was speaking a foreign language. I could not understand her. "What?"

"Joyce is not your mother. She loves you very much, but she isn't your mother."

"Oh," I said, relief flooding through me, "now I see. You mean she's really Georgia Halloran. I knew about that, and about Lorraine Lawrence too. She told me. But she needed those names for Social Security and her driver's license. She was running away, she told me all about it."

"Nina. Please listen to me." But Ruth Boardman walked away from me and stood at the window. "How can I say this to you?" She rubbed her hand over her face and I waited.

By now shivers were passing over my body in waves, my skin was throbbing with terror. Something awful was about to happen, something absolutely terrifying. I knew it. I could feel the impact of what Ruth Board-man was going to say passing from her mind into my own.

"Joyce kidnapped you. She took you out of a hospital in Virginia three days after you were born. Your mother's name is Cynthia Healy. Your father's name is Joe Healy. You have a younger sister too, and her name is Elizabeth. Would you like to see a picture of them?"

I held out my hand and took it. Joyce was not my mother.

My mind felt clear, almost empty now. Objects in the room stood out with perfect clarity. I saw Joyce's sweater on the table and a mug with some tea in it. I saw the kitchen range and our clock which said 7:40. I looked out the window and saw the rose bush bloom-ing by the chain-link fence.

"Will she have to go to jail?" I asked Ruth Board-man. "Can I visit her tonight?"

"Oh, Nina!" Then I looked at Ruth Boardman and realized she was crying. Tears were on her cheeks. Here was this woman, a stranger to me, someone who had tracked us down and caught us, and yet she was crying. It amazed me.

I wanted to stop her. I held up my arm with my palm outstretched like a policeman stopping traffic. The picture I'd been holding fluttered to the table.

It was a small color photograph. A mother and a father were standing outside a doorway with a daughter between them. The daughter was not me though. She was only nine or ten years old. The grass in the picture was very green and the people were wearing summer clothes. They were squinting in the sunshine and smiling. The father was getting bald and you couldn't tell about him, but the other two, the mother and the daughter, both had red hair. That was what struck me. They had red hair.

I picked up the picture and walked over to the window to look at it in the light. It was a small picture, as I said, and you couldn't tell much about specific details like what color the people's eyes were or anything, but I could see that their faces were nice and friendly, and oval rather than round. They look like me, I thought, but without real interest or surprise because they were only people in a photograph.

"Do you want to get washed up?" said Ruth Boardman. "Maybe you should pack a suitcase. We're going to have to leave soon."

By now I knew I wasn't going to see Joyce. She'd been taken away from me, taken out of this apartment probably in handcuffs, and from now on other people, strangers and judges, were going to decide our fate.

"How did you find out where we were?" I asked Ruth Boardman.

"It was the license plates. The garage where you parked your car had them on a list with your address. But we had to make sure and check everything before we arrested Joyce."

I still couldn't understand it. "What about Silky?" I asked.

"Silky?"

"My dog." I said.

"I don't know anything about a dog," she said.

"I'm not going unless I can take Silky." Hearing her name, Silky walked into the kitchen from my room and lay down.

Ruth Boardman petted her a little, but it wasn't really convincing and I could see she wasn't used to dogs. "Fine," she said. "But you better bring a leash. I don't think they allow dogs to run around in the FBI."

I didn't answer or say anything but she went on like I was asking a million questions.

"That's in Manhattan, downtown at Foley Square. The Healys are there. I left them waiting in my office. They flew up from Virginia a few hours ago. Think of them, Nina, the poor people! Everyone was sure you were dead, but they never stopped looking for you.

Every six months they put notices in the papers and checked with us to see if we'd found anything yet. *Every six months!* Most families give up in a few years, but they never did."

I think Ruth Boardman might have been nervous. She'd opened the box of pizza and was eating it piece by piece as she talked.

"Really though, it was Georgia Halloran we had to look for because how could we tell who you were? You were just a baby. But everyone knew it was Georgia Halloran, because the night you disappeared from the hospital so did she. She was working as a nurse on the maternity floor and after that night she never came back. They went to her apartment but she'd moved. The police looked for her everywhere but it was no good, she'd vanished into thin air."

Three whole pieces of pizza were gone. I couldn't believe it. Ruth Boardman looked up and she must have noticed me staring at the box of pizza. "Oh, I'm sorry!" she said. "How rude of me! Don't you want some? I should have asked you."

"No, that's okay. I'm not really hungry." My voice sounded mechanical to me. I wouldn't have been able to chew and swallow. I could barely even lift my feet to walk.

In slow motion I went into my bedroom and pulled the suitcase I always used out of the closet. I looked for my chest too, but it was gone. Maybe they'd let

Joyce take it. The last time I'd checked, the money was still there. We were using it to live on, so there was less than before, but plenty still.

The lock to the chest had gotten lost a few weeks ago and I'd taken out all my stuff. Joyce hadn't even said anything. My glass animals were in my jewelry box now, along with the crescent moon earrings and Sam Gordon's letter. It had his return address on it. Maybe I could write him now. But I'd say we'd moved to Virginia permanently, that my mother had gotten a really good job there.

I put the jewelry box into my suitcase first and then I loaded in a bunch of clothes, whatever I grabbed in the closet, hangers and all. I thought about taking my sunset collage, but I decided against it. Let whoever moved here next wonder about it. Maybe if they had a kid, she'd like to see those suns setting over mountains and rivers and oceans across the world.

But I packed my little painting, *Cows at Sunset*. It was one of the best things Joyce had ever given me. I remembered the happiness in her face as she'd watched me unwrap it, and the colors in the painting jumped and spun as my eyes blurred with tears.

"Ready now?" Ruth Boardman was standing at the door of my room. She pretended not to notice I'd been crying. I think she must have straightened up the kitchen because the pizza box was gone and Joyce's mug and the teapot were in the sink. "Don't forget Silky's leash," she said.

"I want to check the backyard," I said. "Just to make sure that I have everything."

Actually I wanted to say good-bye to Laurel, I didn't want to just vanish on her. Good, she was playing under the grape arbor. She'd started coming over after supper sometimes. I'd told her that it was okay, to come over whenever she wanted.

"Hey, Laurel. I came to say good-bye. We're moving again." I sat down next to her.

"Where are you going?"

"Somewhere great—Virginia. It never gets cold there, this is the coldest it gets."

"You're lucky," said Laurel. "Can I still come over even if you're not here?"

"Sure. If it's okay with your mother."

"I'll go ask her," she said and she squeezed through the gap in the fence and ran into her house.

In my house Ruth Boardman was waiting. I took my suitcase and kneeled to hook Silky's leash onto her collar. That's when I saw Joyce's pocketbook. It was on the floor under the kitchen table. "Never go anywhere without your pocketbook," she always used to say. She kept her makeup in it and everything else. How was she going to be able to get along without it?

I guess I could have said something to Ruth Boardman, but I didn't want to ask her any favors. I didn't even want to mention Joyce's name.

As I walked out the door, images of the two of us began flying through my mind. A merry-go-round in a park, Joyce watching me and smiling as she stood at the railing. Six in the morning, breakfast in a diner in Montana, horses tied up outside.

Faster and faster the images came as I drove with Ruth Boardman through the New York traffic to where the people who'd come to claim me were waiting. A walk through a field. A ride in an elevator. Coming home from school. Crying in Joyce's arms.

"Take it easy, kiddo," she whispered. It was her voice. I swear it.

↙ Part Five

Virginia Beach, Virginia

20 They let me keep my name, at least I had that. The baby had been named Jessica, but I was not her. She was no one, a tiny little helpless creature who'd vanished when she was three days old and never came back again.

It took me a long time to make the Healys understand why I wanted to still be myself, *Nina.* Maybe they don't even understand now, but at least they're not trying to smother me with love anymore. I couldn't take that!

The moment they saw me in Ruth Boardman's office, they'd rushed at me with their arms open, all three of them. It was one of the scariest things that ever happened to me. Imagine three strangers, grabbing you like they own you and screaming and crying and wetting your face with their tears. I'm not really blaming them, but the way I was feeling then, it set me back. It made me feel like I had to protect myself against them.

Since that time they've tried to make me feel at home every way they could. Even though they never had any pets before, they're been really enthusiastic about Silky. I have a big room of my own with white ruffled curtains and a view of the house across the street. I get fifteen dollars a week allowance, and now that I have my driver's license, they let me drive the car.

It's been good to realize I'm not going to have to move right away and good to stay in the same school for two years and really get to know some kids, but I still don't feel like I belong here.

Everything in Virginia Beach is colonial. Our house is a brick colonial with two pillars out in front and a fireplace and a curving stairway in the front hall. It's in a development called King's Grant and our school is named First Colonial. I guess a lot of history took place on the Virginia shore but you can't really see it now. All the buildings look brand-new.

This is a rich town and nothing bad ever seems to happen to anyone. Maybe that's why Joe and Cindy never like to hear me speak of the past. "Don't let's talk about that," they'd say whenever I brought up some fact about Joyce or something we'd done together. "Haven't we all had enough pain?" they'd say if I persisted, which I did quite a lot, at first.

Cindy would walk out of the room and Joe would put his arm around me and shake his head a few times, but in a sad way, not like he was angry. And later on, maybe when I was getting ready for bed, Elizabeth would come into my room and say, "You shouldn't do that to Mommy and Daddy. It really hurts their feelings."

So in the end Elizabeth was the one I talked to. She was the one who told me how it had been in her family when I was away with Joyce. About the phone calls they'd gotten from strange people claiming to know where the baby was, and the footprints that had come from morgues whenever a child's corpse was found and the relief each time when they didn't match the ones that the hospital had.

I can't imagine how Elizabeth knew about this. Mostly I think she was a good spy. And of course it affected her. "They had me to make up for you," she told me one day when we were riding our bikes. "I never would have been born if you weren't kidnapped."

"Don't be dumb," I said. "I'm sure they wanted more than one kid."

"Well why didn't they have any more after me then?" Elizabeth asked, pulling her hair out of her eyes and pedaling hard.

I had no answer for this.

Joe Healy ran one of the shipyards in Virginia Beach and Cindy was the bookkeeper there, so that meant that Elizabeth and I were on our own when we got home from school in the afternoon. We weren't the only ones though. This was common in our neighborhood, even though the houses were big and roomy and the wives didn't have to work. Kids as young as six and seven were left rattling around in the houses alone. At least Elizabeth and I had each other.

The first thing I always did when I got home was to check the mailbox. Joyce was allowed to write me from prison and she usually wrote every week. She was in Alderson, West Virginia, about three hundred miles away.

Her letters were even matter-of-fact and sometimes even funny. She'd tell me prison jokes. Question: "What's a nice girl like you doing in a place like this?" Answer: "Time." But I thought that below the surface she must be lonely. Her letters always said she missed me and they were signed with a line of XXXXs and OOOOs for hugs and kisses.

I think the prison might have checked the mail, because Joyce never said anything really controversial in her letters and once when I'd sent her some wild-flowers I'd pressed, she wrote back saying she wasn't allowed to receive *anything* ("anything" was underlined) except the letter itself.

I told her about high school and I described our neighborhood and the Healys' house, but I never ac-

tually told her what living here was like. It might have
hurt her feelings, and that was the last thing I wanted.

But recently we'd begun to write each other about
the possibility of me going to visit her in prison. "It's
not bad," she wrote. "They give us all day, as much
time as we need, and we're allowed to sit outside on
the grass with our visitors if the weather is nice. Why
don't you come in the early fall? It's nice here then,
not too hot and not too cold."

Who else might have visited her? Maybe she really
did have parents who were alive or brothers or sisters.
That was one thing I wanted to ask Joyce if I went to
see her. But I was scared to bring up the idea to Cindy
and Joe. They knew Joyce and I wrote each other, but
it seemed impossible that they'd let me go see her—
in Alderson, in a prison. Because she'd pleaded guilty,
there never even was a trial. She'd been sentenced to
twenty years.

I told myself I could wait until I was eighteen, then
I wouldn't be a minor anymore and I could do what I
wanted. But a week after my sixteenth birthday, I got
the saddest letter from Joyce.

Dear Nina,

*Your birthday was last Tuesday. I thought about
you all day long. Do you remember when you turned
thirteen? We were living in Montpelier then and I
made you an angel food cake. The funny thing was,
at dinner in the cafeteria Tuesday, they had angel*

food cake set out on the food trays for dessert. I took
one look at it and started bawling. A big mistake. It's
best to act tough here. If you don't, you're in for
trouble. I hope you had a nice birthday. What did
you do? Did you get any good presents? Write me
soon.

Love,
Joyce

This was the first time she'd given me a glimpse of
what it must really be like to be in prison. It really
upset me. The past six months or so, Joyce had been
receding from my thoughts a little, but after that letter,
I began thinking about her all the time again. I knew
I had to get to Alderson and visit her, and finally I
decided to ask Elizabeth how I should go about it.

Unlike Joe and Cindy, she loved to hear about my
life with Joyce. She knew all the places we'd ever lived.
Some afternoons we'd pull the big atlas down from the
bookcase and lie on the living room floor and I'd trace
our journeys for her, the roads we took and the things
we did along the way. I could confide in Elizabeth.
Even though she was three years younger than me, I'd
say she was the closest person I'd ever had as a friend.
We weren't like sisters at all.

"Ask Daddy to take you to see Joyce," she told me.
"Show him the letter and tell him that it's really important. But don't say anything to Mommy. Let Daddy
tell her."

According to Elizabeth, the reason Joe and Cindy agreed was that they felt sorry for Joyce because they'd been sad on all my birthdays too. But *I* think they just wanted to satisfy me about seeing her. They didn't know what else they could give me that I didn't have.

Something Joe Healy said to me in the car as we were coming into Alderson made me realize they still had hopes for me, that I'd finally change and love them. "Maybe after today you'll be able to say good-bye to Joyce," he said. "I don't think you ever really got a chance to say good-bye."

We'd left Virginia Beach at noon on Saturday and made arrangements to stay overnight in a guest house in town. The prison knew I was coming, they had my name on a list. Joe would take me there on Sunday morning. Alderson was out in the middle of nowhere. The lady who ran the guest house said that almost all her customers came to visit prisoners. It was like the town existed only because the prison did.

It was kind of a mournful place too. All night long trains went by, blowing their whistles. It kept me awake, not that I would have gotten much sleep anyway. I was too excited.

I almost felt the way I used to feel about going to meet a boyfriend. I hadn't really had any boyfriends in Virginia Beach, but, say, like when I was seeing Daryl Carpenter in Logan. It was that same intense sensation, like you just can't wait to find out what's going to happen.

Joe and I had breakfast at the guest house and then at ten he dropped me off. A guard at the gate checked my name and another guard took me into a long, high-ceilinged room to wait for Joyce. They were going to call her at the cottage where she lived.

It was early November. I'd remembered what she said about sitting outside if the weather was nice, and I'd brought along a quilted Chinese jacket I had in case it got cooler as the morning went on. Here's what I was wearing: a dark blue corduroy skirt, black flats, and a purple cotton sweater with full sleeves. My hair was almost shoulder-length now and I'd had it permed so it stood out from my head and was curly. I'd stopped wearing makeup (even though other kids in Virginia Beach wore a lot) and I had on my crescent moon earrings.

It seemed like they were taking a long time to bring Joyce. I stood at one of the windows in the room looking out onto the grounds of the prison. Red brick buildings, two stories high, were arranged in a purposeful way on big rolling lawns. There were no bars anywhere, but the window I was looking through had wire mesh in the glass and all around there was a chain-link fence twelve feet high with strands of barbed wire on top. I'd wanted to feel that the place Joyce had been during these two years wasn't bad, but I couldn't feel that. This place was awful.

"Is that you, Nina?"

I turned around slowly, afraid suddenly to see her. We were meeting in a prison and suddenly the fact of her crime came down like a rock between us. We'd never referred to it in our letters or called it by its name, *kidnapping*.

Joyce smiled at me and held out her hand. "You look beautiful," she said. "What a beautiful girl."

I couldn't answer. I was overwhelmed by the sight of her, how familiar she seemed and yet strange too. It was almost as if there were two people there, the one I knew and someone I'd never known at all.

Of course she looked different too. Her hair wasn't blonde anymore or even red. She'd let it go gray and her face seemed softer. You could tell that her skin was breaking down in lines, but you wanted to run your fingers over the soft surface. I think she'd lost weight. She was wearing her cherry-red skirt and sweater that I remembered from before.

"You look good too," I said. "They must let you wear your own clothes here."

"Yes, but this and three or four other things are all I have left. They make you feel privileged to wear your own clothes."

"Can't you buy new ones?" I asked.

"If you want to, I guess."

Conversation seemed like an enormous effort. I thought something about the room we were in might be the problem. The ceiling was really high, as I said, and there were little groups of wooden chairs arranged on the wooden floor. It was a big room, almost like a hall or an auditorium, but nobody was in it except us.

"Could we go outside?" I asked.

"I'd like that," said Joyce. She took my arm as we walked past the guard. I wasn't sure whether it was to protect me or herself, but I was glad to be closer to her. Outdoors there was much more of a feeling of freedom. Clouds were moving quickly across the sky. The weather kept changing, warm when the sun was out and cool when it wasn't.

We sat down next to a flower bed and for a long time neither of us said anything. Then from out of nowhere it seemed, Joyce said to me, "Aren't those the earrings Lionel Winter made? The ones you told me about in Venice?"

I reached my hands up to my ears, trying to cover up the earrings or at least stop them from tinkling.

"No, let me see." She moved closer to me and cupped one in her palm. "Lionel used to be in love with me," she said. "It's so odd you met him."

The wind began to blow, flattening the grass. I put my jacket on.

"You must have a lot of questions, things you want to know about the past," said Joyce.

"Not really," I said. "Not unless you want to tell me."

"That money you found . . . did you really think I stole it?"

I shrugged. I didn't know why she'd brought that up when it was the last thing that would matter to me now.

"Well, I didn't. It was some money my grandmother left me. My parents wired it to me when we were still in Logan. I always told them where I was and they knew what I'd done too." Joyce sounded almost defiant, like she was daring me to argue with her.

I felt really sad and nervous. I'd never meant to wound her in any way or make her relive painful times. She seemed in enough pain as it was. You could tell it in her posture and the way she sat, tense and guarded, with her eyes on me.

I looked around. More people had come outside now and they were sitting in groups on the lawn, visiting. There were men and women together and whole families, some with little children. At least I was sixteen now. Imagine being in first grade or kindergarten and having to visit your mother in a federal women's prison.

"But there must be something good about being here," I said. "One thing that's all right. What about friends? Don't you have any?" I think I sounded upset and I hadn't wanted to, but I couldn't help it.

"Not real friends," said Joyce. "But that's okay, it's a prison. They're punishing you. 'Count time, ladies,' they say, and then they line you up and count you nine times a day. They want to weaken people and keep you separate, so that you won't be so dangerous to them. But lots of times the prisoners are worse than the guards anyway."

My stomach began churning. For a while neither of us spoke. A train went by, screeching its brakes around a turn. Maybe it was like the trains I'd heard in town the night before, but here it sounded much louder. Joyce smiled and shrugged her shoulders and we waited until the noise vanished far away in the distance.

"The longest ones are at night. At first they wake you up over and over as they come by. You can feel the ground shake under your bed. But after a few weeks you don't even hear them."

"Are they passenger trains?" I asked.

"No, coal trains. They're taking the coal out of the mountains." She kneeled as if she were going to stand up, but then she sat down again. "Do you remember when we lived in Dubuque?" she said. "How you loved the trains?"

Actually I'd forgotten that particular thing about Dubuque, but it was true. There were railroad tracks at the end of our street and we knew when the freight trains passed. There was one at two-thirty and one at four and one at midnight. You could almost tell time by them. Occasionally Joyce would let me stay up until midnight just to hear the train. Once we'd walked to the tracks so we could see it in the moonlight.

I closed my eyes and for an instant it was as if that train were before me again, white and ghostly, rocketing along the tracks. Joyce had thought it would be exciting for me to see it, but really I'd been terrified.

She was beginning to cry. "Everything I ever did was for you. You know that, Nina."

"I know."

Our true feelings had jumped into focus so abruptly! I took her hand and moved closer to her in the grass.

"You were so lovely when you were born. Just the smell of you in my arms and the way you looked up at me as if I was someone familiar, someone you'd always known. And it was really quiet and peaceful in the hospital at night with only the two of us. Was it a crime that I loved you? I never meant to take you. I didn't *plan* it."

She turned her head to the ground. Tears ran from her eyes. "Can you ever forgive me?" she whispered.

I petted her shoulder and couldn't speak. I wanted to give the right answer. I didn't want to cry. "I don't know what you're talking about," I said. "There's nothing to forgive. You brought me up. You were my mother."

"But all those years—"

"They were good," I told her. "We had an exciting life."

"Really?" She was wiping her face off with the back of her hand. I wished I had a tissue to give her.

"Sure," I said. "After the things we did, real life is enough to put you to sleep."

But then for some reason I started talking about it. I think I just wanted her to know about Virginia Beach so she could picture my life if she wanted to. I told her about the Healys, not really about living with them, but just what kind of people they were in general. I described what we did on weekends, our trips to the beach and a trip we'd taken last spring to Washington, D.C.

Joyce listened but she didn't say much. Around us people had begun standing up and moving toward a big building down a hill. I thought probably they were going to have lunch. A clock was striking.

I got to my feet too, scared of what I had to say next. "I . . . I have to go now. Joe Healy is waiting for me outside. I'm supposed to meet him at the gate at twelve."

Joyce laughed, a funny nervous laugh. "That's okay. Don't worry. We have to go into the cafeteria anyway. They count us there." She held my face between her hands and looked at me for a long time. "I love you, Nina. It was good you came."

And then before I could answer or stop her, she followed the other prisoners and visitors across the lawn.